"The moonlight must be influencing you again."

She bantered, more tremulous than confused.

"I never let the moonlight influence me," he denied huskily, his thickly lashed eyes locking inescapably with hers. Then almost immediately he groaned, "But—oh, hell! Why did you have to come here tonight?" He cupped her face between both hands, and his lips came down on hers with a devastating insistence.

Currents of fire immediately coursed through Rowan, scattering her senses and weakening her inhibitions and provoking a response she was unable to control.

Fraser's mouth caught the sensitive cord at the side of her arching throat, the tip of his tongue teasing her to throbbing heights. And then with a smothered exclamation he swept her into his arms and began carrying her toward the house....

Books by Kerry Allyne

HARLEQUIN ROMANCES

HARLEQUIN PRESENTS

These books may be available at your local bookseller.

For a free catalog listing all titles currently available,
send your name and address to:

Harlequin Reader Service
P.O. Box 52040, Phoenix, AZ 85072-9988
Canadian address: Stratford, Ontario N5A 6W2

Somewhere to Call Home

Kerry Allyne

Harlequin Books

TORONTO • NEW YORK • LONDON
AMSTERDAM • PARIS • SYDNEY • HAMBURG
STOCKHOLM • ATHENS • TOKYO • MILAN

Original hardcover edition published in 1983
by Mills & Boon Limited

ISBN 0-373-02593-9

Harlequin Romance first edition January 1984

CHAPTER ONE

Rowan Adams abruptly pushed herself into a sitting position on her brightly coloured beach towel and gave her friend Tanya an appalled look. 'No! No way!' she refused with a grimaced half laugh. 'You and Evan can work out your own problems, but don't include me.' Her wide, curving mouth formed a rueful moue. 'Besides, what makes you think his overbearing cousin would fall for such a ruse? In case it's skipped your notice, he and I haven't exactly hit it off the few times we've come in contact with one another.'

'Only because you seemed determined to rile him in any way possible, otherwise I'm sure it would have been different,' Tanya impressed earnestly as she too sat up. Her blue eyes surveyed her companion knowledgeably. She knew from past experience that Rowan's long wheat-gold hair, velvety brown eyes, slender tip-tilted nose, and invitingly shaped mouth acted like a magnet to most members of the opposite sex, and it usually required very little effort on her friend's part to have them willingly succumbing to her every whim. Not that their attentions had ever made Rowan vain, though, she had to admit, because she appeared to regard it as a somewhat whimsical joke that after languishing, unwanted, in an orphanage for all but nine months of her first sixteen years of life, she should now have so many people only too anxious to acknowledge her existence.

'Perhaps,' Rowan shrugged indifferently, brushing

sand from her shapely legs. 'But in any event, *I've* no wish to find out.'

'Oh, please! Couldn't you just try ... for—for my sake?' Tanya resorted to pleading in persuasive tones. 'You know tonight will more than likely be the last time I'll see Evan,' referring to the fact that their jobs as casual waitresses at the resort hotel would be coming to an end after that day's evening meal, now that the height of the summer season had passed and the school holidays were over, 'and we do so just want to spend it on our own.'

'Then why doesn't Evan do something to keep his cousin from interfering?'

'Because we—well, I,' Tanya amended a trifle sheepishly, 'thought Fraser would be less suspicious this way. You know he's been watching Evan's every movement like a hawk.'

'In order to keep him from becoming too involved with someone he regards as a socially unconnected nobody?' Rowan propounded contemptuously. Tanya had spent eight years at the orphanage too.

Her friend hunched one shoulder awkwardly. 'I—well, that could be part of it, I guess. He certainly didn't approve of the—er—somewhat noisy parties the casual hotel staff have had on the beach at times, did he?'

Didn't approve! As Rowan remembered it, Fraser Delaney had been absolutely *furious*, and not only because of the loud music and general sounds of hilarity which had more often than not accompanied their parties, but also because the grounds of his private beach house had been inadvertently—or, at least harmlessly, she corrected honestly—intruded upon.

'And that's supposed to be reason enough for trying to stop his precious cousin from being contaminated by your presence, is it?' she flared aloud. 'It would serve him right if you were really serious about your relationship with Evan.' Then, on noting her friend's ensuing change of expression, she frowned, 'You're not, are you?'

Tanya pressed her lips together and then smiled, apologetically almost. 'More than I intended to be at the outset,' she nodded.

'Oh, hell!' Rowan partly groaned, partly laughed. 'Here we go again! You fall in and out of love faster and more often than anyone else I've ever heard of!'

'Mmm, I know, but this time I honestly think it's the real thing,' Tanya smiled with her.

'I've heard you say that before!'

'I know that too, but with Evan I feel different somehow.'

Leaning back, Rowan reclined on her elbows. 'And Evan? How does he feel?' she just had to enquire.

'The same . . . I think,' Tanya answered hesitantly. 'That's why I wanted to ensure we had this last evening alone together,' she went on in an urgent voice. 'To try and discover exactly how he feels about *me*. I figure, if he's serious, then he'll be bound to say something, since we're supposed to be leaving in the morning.'

'*Supposed* to be leaving?' Rowan immediately queried. 'I thought it was all settled and we *were* leaving in the morning?'

Tanya shifted a little uncomfortably. 'Yes, well, I know that's what we said we'd do, but I thought that if Evan does—does . . .'

'Reciprocate your regard?' offered Rowan, wryly helpful.

'Something like that,' with a grin. 'And that being the case, I was sort of hoping that instead of heading further north along the coast looking for work, maybe we could try for something else around here.' Her eyes sought Rowan's anxiously. 'You wouldn't mind, would you? I mean, it's not as if we have anything in particular to go north for. We were really only following the sun, weren't we?'

'Because we figured that if we had to be out of work, it was better to be so in a warm climate than a cold one,' Rowan felt obliged to remind her drily.

'Well, you could hardly call the north coast of New South Wales cold!'

'No, maybe not, but you seem to have forgotten we've been trying for the last two weeks to find other work here in Kurrawa Bay, but to date have come up with precisely zilch.'

Tanya pulled a disconsolate face. 'Oh, well, if Evan can't shake off his cousin later tonight it won't matter anyway,' she sighed. 'I may as well admit the inevitable and accept that we'll be on our way again tomorrow.'

Rowan rolled on to her side, supporting her head on her hand, a thoughtful furrow creasing her forehead. 'Couldn't Evan arrange for a fake phone call saying Fraser's presence was required back at the farm, or something?' Since the Delaneys' macadamia plantation was apparently only some thirty or forty kilometres inland, it seemed a reasonable suggestion to her.

However, Tanya shook her head disappointedly. 'Not really, I'm afraid. You see, from what Evan tells me, about the only thing that would recall them— apart from extremely adverse weather, of course— would be a breakdown at the processing factory that the mechanic couldn't fix, and as the factory is Evan's domain then he'd be the one who had to leave, not Fraser.'

'That's no good, then, is it?' Rowan wrinkled her nose in disgust and lay absently contemplating the other suntanned occupants of the beach for a moment. 'Well, how about an invitation to a supposed party at the Kurrawa Bay Hotel? He's great mates with the owner from what I hear, so that would sound quite feasible.'

'Too feasible,' Tanya couldn't help laughing. 'That's exactly what and where he and Evan are supposed to be going to this evening.'

'Oh! But without you, I presume?' Rowan's lips thinned angrily.

'Without me,' came the doleful confirmation.

'The unbelievable arrogance of the man!' Rowan exploded fiercely, coming upright again and clasping her arms about her updrawn knees. 'Just who does he think he is, trying to stop you from seeing his damned cousin?' If he'd bothered to get to know Tanya he would have found she was one of the sweetest-natured persons imaginable, she fumed inwardly. 'But if that's the way he wants to play it, then okay, we'll have to see if we can't really give him something to worry about, won't we?'

'Such as?' Tanya quizzed tentatively, but on a note of rising hope for all that.

'Such as, where you and Evan have disappeared to tonight!'

'You mean you'll do it, after all?' Tanya gasped delightedly. 'You'll keep Fraser occupied so Evan can slip away to meet me?'

'I will!' was the determinedly nodded answer. Although, as a picture of Evan's cousin flashed into Rowan's mind, she immediately qualified the remark with a slightly more judicious, 'Well, I'll certainly do my best.' At thirty-two, Fraser Delaney was ten years older than his cousin, and their brief encounters so far had left her with the distinct impression that he wasn't a man to be either easily swayed or underestimated—and especially not by any female!

'Oh, I haven't any doubts at all that you'll succeed,' beamed Tanya confidently, her eyes bright with gratitude. 'So where will you approach him? When they reach the hotel?'

Deep in thought, Rowan shook her head slowly. 'No, I don't think so. Since he knows so many people here at the Bay there's always the likelihood of too many interruptions for me to keep him distracted as to Evan's whereabouts for very long. It might be better if I waylaid him at the beach house before they leave.'

'Beard the lion in his den, so to speak?' grinned Tanya.

'I could have wished you hadn't put it quite like that,' Rowan retorted with a wryly expressive smile of her own. Now that the heat of the moment had passed, some of her previous doubts concerning the scheme were beginning to return. 'But yes, I suppose in a way that's what I will be doing. I would have preferred it otherwise, of course, but it doesn't appear as if I've any choice. Anywhere more public and I may not even get to first base.' Her lips twitched irrepressibly. 'As I said before, he and I have been rather more on glaring than speaking terms up until now, so there's always the possibility he may refuse to talk to me at all.'

Tanya glanced at her worriedly. 'It's not likely, though . . . is it?'

Rowan's smoothly arched brows peaked sardonically. 'Who can say with someone as autocratic as Fraser Delaney,' she grimaced. 'But he doesn't take kindly to outspoken females, I can tell you that. In fact, it wouldn't surprise me if he didn't take to *any* females at all. No wonder he's not married. Probably no woman wants him!'

The acidly voiced conjecture had Tanya forgetting her problems momentarily and giving way to laughter. 'Oh, you can't possibly believe that,' she gurgled in no little amusement. 'Even though he's trying to keep Evan and me apart, that doesn't make me blind to the man's undeniable magnetism, and you know as well as I do that there isn't an unmarried girl in Kurrawa Bay—and some of the married ones too, I suspect— who wouldn't be over the moon if they could only manage to catch his attention. Why, even since we've been here, on those occasions when he has taken someone out, I don't think it's ever been the same female twice in a row.'

'It no doubt being a case of "once bitten, twice shy"!' The sarcasm in Rowan's tone became even more pronounced.

'For them . . . or him?' put in Tanya drily.

A grudging smile made its appearance. 'All right, so he's not the least attractive male around,' which was as far as Rowan was prepared to concede, 'but that still doesn't alter anything with regard to this evening. When he sees who's come calling . . .' She didn't bother to finish the sentence but just hunched one smooth, tanned shoulder explicitly.

'Oh, you can do it, Rowan, I know you can!' her friend promptly assured her.

'Hmm . . . I wish I was as certain as you are.' Then, after a time spent staring at the sparkling, thundering surf a few metres away, 'You'll have to get in touch with Evan somehow, you know, so he's aware he's supposed to make good his—umm—escape as soon as I arrive.'

'Don't worry, I'll find some way of contacting him without Fraser knowing.'

'So how long do you expect me to keep him occupied? Half an hour, three-quarters?'

Tanya considered the matter carefully. 'Well, I really think it ought to be an hour at least, to be on the safe side.'

'An hour ... *at least!*' Rowan's widening brown eyes registered her dismay at the suggestion. 'Have you any idea just how long that is when you're struggling to be nice to someone you don't even like? Good lord, what do you expect me to say to the man that's going to keep him diverted for that length of time?'

'Knowing you, you'll think of something.' Tanya obviously had every confidence in her, even if she hadn't. 'I've rarely seen you lost for words.'

'A circumstance Matron Willis at the orphanage was fond of predicting would rebound on me one of these days,' Rowan recalled ironically. She gave a light, although not altogether easy, laugh. 'You don't suppose she's about to be proved right, do you?'

'No, of course not. Why should she be? She was always forecasting that every one of us would get into trouble for something or other, but I can't honestly remember any of her predictions coming true.'

'No, I guess not,' Rowan acceded on a sigh. But feeling strangely restless all of a sudden, she dropped her wide-brimmed sunhat on to her towel and began fashioning her hair into a ponytail with the aid of a rubber band. This completed, she rose gracefully to her feet, her slender but perfectly proportioned figure, covered only by a golden yellow bikini which made her suntan appear even darker than it actually was, drawing just about every male glance her way as she looked down at her companion to propose, 'How about a last swim before we have to head back to the hotel for our shift?'

Nodding an enthusiastic acquiescence, Tanya joined her quickly, and in silence they made their way down to the water's edge. Both their minds were independently engaged with thoughts of the coming evening.

Fortunately for Rowan and Tanya, now that the hotel wasn't quite so crowded, they were able to finish their shift a little earlier than usual that night, and shortly afterwards Rowan was hurrying along the Esplanade towards the Delaneys' beach house while Tanya waited anxiously at the hotel.

Dressed in a slim-fitting dress of black and watermelon pink superfine cotton with a self-patterned tie belt, and tiny ribbon shoulder straps to support the flatteringly low bodice, Rowan knew she looked her best, although that didn't prevent the nervous fluttering of butterflies in her stomach as she neared her objective. It was the first time she had ever attempted anything like this and, her friend's assurances to the contrary, she wasn't at all certain she could carry it off successfully. In fact, she was half hoping Fraser and Evan had already left the house.

Five minutes later, though, after leaving the precincts of the town behind—even with its increasing popularity, Kurrawa Bay still wasn't a particularly large resort—and heading towards the private residences which sporadically dotted the foreshore, she could see lights shining from the Delaney house and her rising hopes were forced to take a downward plunge. By the time she had reached the neat, white-painted cottage, however, the lights had all been extinguished, and as she headed up the flagstone path to the front door she met both Evan and his cousin coming down the verandah steps towards her.

'Rowan!' Evan immediately injected a note of surprise into his voice. 'What brings you out this way? Did you want to see me about something?' And without giving her an opportunity to answer, 'Oh, sorry, I don't think you've actually been introduced to my cousin yet, have you? Rowan Adams—Fraser Delaney. Rowan's Tanya Robinson's friend,' he explained to the man beside him.

Fraser acknowledged the introduction with a cool, discouraging nod. 'I know . . . we've met,' he advised curtly.

'Y-yes,' agreed Rowan shakily, then went on quickly while the chance still presented itself. 'And—and that's what I came to see you about.'

'Oh?'

The patently uninterested note in his voice had Rowan swallowing in despair. 'Well . . . yes.' She looked at Evan as if slightly embarrassed by his presence and back to his cousin again. 'Er—could we go inside, do you think?' indicating the house behind them with a hopefully persuasive glance.

In the fitful light of the moon—there were no street lights along this secluded part of the bay—it was impossible for her to see his expression or to judge his reaction to her request. He merely appeared as a tall, dark, and rather overwhelming shape towering above her, and she waited nervously for his reply. If he refused she didn't know how she was going to separate him from Evan.

Apparently Evan must have thought the same, because he promptly offered, 'I'll wait out here for you, Fraser.'

'There's no need,' his cousin finally revealed his thoughts on the matter, and in the same indifferent tone. 'I can't think of anything that . . .'

'Please . . .!' Rowan broke in on him as imploringly as she was able. It really went against the grain when his uncompromising attitude was beginning to make her temper rise. If it wasn't for Tanya she would have told him just where he could go!

'Well, you could at least listen now that she's walked all the way out here,' urged Evan, doing his bit to help.

'It's only half a kilometre,' Fraser belittled the distance sardonically, and aggravating Rowan even further.

'She still made the effort,' Evan pointed out.

Fraser turned slowly to look at him. 'And you seem very anxious for me to comply. Any particular reason why?' he questioned softly.

'Of course not,' came the laughing denial with an inherent innocence that Rowan only wished she could emulate. 'I haven't spoken to Rowan since Wednesday, so how could I possibly know what she wants to say to you?'

How indeed! Apart from her opening, she didn't have any idea herself yet!

'It won't take long,' Rowan herself now joined in to assure him, albeit not very truthfully in view of the length of time Tanya suggested it should take, but feeling obligated to do the best she could on her friend's behalf all the same. If ever called upon, she knew Tanya would willingly do the same for her.

'Go on! I'll wait for you,' offered Evan again.

'No, you go on ahead. I'll catch up with you in town,' said Fraser calmly, and had Rowan successively almost gasping her astonishment out loud, and then gleefully hiding her delight at the turn the matter had taken. She had fully expected Fraser to insist on his cousin waiting for him.

'Right you are. I'll see you later, then.' Needing no second bidding, Evan, with an imperceptible half wink in Rowan's direction, was on his way to town before anyone could say another word.

'So what was it you wanted to say to me ... in private?' Fraser's voice abruptly cut into the ensuing silence.

The unmistakable sarcasm it contained had Rowan both flushing selfconsciously and gritting her teeth to avoid answering as she would have liked. 'Couldn't we— er—still go inside?' she suggested instead with a credibly demure smile. If she was supposed to distract him with her looks as Tanya had proposed, she mused wryly, she would have more chance of doing so inside where he could see her, than outside in the dark. 'I— I've been on my feet since four this afternoon and I'd rather sit down, if you don't mind.'

With what could only be described as an indifferent shrug, Fraser began mounting the steps, but obviously unable to refrain from reminding in a subtle drawl, 'I thought you said it wouldn't take long.'

'No, well, I'd still prefer to sit ... unless you have any objections, of course.' Rowan couldn't prevent an edge of sarcasm creeping into her own voice as she followed him across the verandah.

'Not at all.' Fraser inclined his head sardonically and, pushing open the door, turned on the inside lights before standing back and allowing her to precede him.

As she entered, Rowan's eyes swept round the softly lit room quickly. Noting the warmly glowing polished parquet flooring; the tropical look of the neatly arranged cane furniture; some not so orderly book- shelves along one wall containing a variety of clearly well-used books and magazines; a mosaic-tiled bar near the large, sliding glass windows which led on to the verandah facing the beach, and which Fraser was now in the act of opening, letting in the sounds of whirring cicadas and the ever-present rhythmic pounding of the sea.

'Have a seat,' he invited—facetiously, she suspected—indicating a floral cushioned two-seater sofa, but choosing one of the leather padded bar stools for himself.

Actually, now that she was inside and could see him more clearly—and his decidedly unco-operative expression!—Rowan was sure she would have felt at less of a disadvantage if she remained standing, but she guessed she didn't really have a choice, so she sank down on to the sofa with a sigh, presenting an attractive length of her shapely tanned legs as she crossed them.

'What a pleasant room this is,' she commented brightly, trying to waste time in any manner possible. 'Have you owned the house for long?'

'Some years.'

Rowan allowed neither the downturn of his mouth or his uncommunicativeness to put her off. 'And you and Evan always come here for your holidays, do you?'

'Not always, no.'

She looked around the room again, as much to escape the disturbingly direct gaze of his thickly lashed eyes as anything. 'Do you ever lease it?' she chose to ask next.

'Why? Are you looking for a house to rent?' he countered on an ironic note.

'Oh, no,' she made herself laugh, even though she felt more like slapping him. 'Besides, we could never afford to rent anything like this. I was just wondering, that's all.'

'Why?'

'Why?' she repeated blankly. That was the last thing she'd expected him to ask. 'Well, because I—I was just interested, I suppose.'

'In assessing Evan's assets on your friend's behalf?' he gibed.

'No!' Her brown eyes flashed furiously, instinctively. 'And don't you dare suggest Tanya's so mercenary! I'll have you know that some of us fortunately consider there's more to life than the mere amassing of wealth!'

His shapely mouth tilted wryly. 'You make it sound like a dirty word.'

With her attention caught by the unexpected curve of his lips, Rowan disconcertingly found herself suddenly aware of him as a man, and not just someone she was there to detain for a while. It was almost as if she was seeing him for the first time as she surveyed the dark brown hair that tended to curl forward on to his broad forehead, the laughter lines she had never noticed before radiating out from his glossily framed grey eyes, the attractively straight nose above that sensuously moulded mouth, and a jaw which told of a resolute inner strength.

Clad in a pair of dark blue pants and a paler blue silk knit shirt, he appeared both casual and relaxed as he leant back with his elbows resting on the bar behind him, but at the same time his wide-framed and muscular form somehow managed to convey the impression there was an underlying watchfulness that could surface with devastating speed should the need arise. A notion which promptly had her thoughts returning to the matter at hand and surmising she was hardly likely to meet with any success at all if she continued arguing with him.

She looked down at her fingers clenched tightly in her lap and then sent him a studiously contrite glance from beneath her long, curling lashes. 'I'm sorry,' she apologised huskily. 'I was really only trying to convince you that nothing is farther from Tanya's mind.'

'Or yours either?' One well-defined brow quirked upwards.

'Or mine either,' she almost snapped, but just managed to soften her words to a dulcet agreement in time.

Fraser didn't immediately comment, but sat appraising her silently until Rowan thought her nerves couldn't stand the strain any more. 'Well?' he eventually quizzed, mockingly.

'W-well ... what?' She stared at him in some confusion.

His slate grey eyes held hers relentlessly. 'Unless I'm very much mistaken, you haven't yet explained why you're here,' he drawled.

'Oh!' Rowan could feel her cheeks colouring beneath his unwavering gaze. 'Yes—well, actually . . .' Halting, she sought to waste more time by swallowing as if her throat was dry and asking limpidly, 'Do you think I could have a drink, please? It's very warm tonight, isn't it?' waving a hand in front of her face.

'I hadn't noticed,' he returned drily, but to her relief rising to his feet and rounding the end of the bar. 'What would you like?'

'A—a gin and lemon will do fine, if you have it, please.' She suspected some fortification might not go amiss.

Fraser retrieved two glassses from beneath the bar, dropped ice into each, and then poured Rowan's drink before splashing some whisky into the other glass for himself. Leaving the second one on the counter, he carried hers across to her.

'Thank you,' she accepted it from him uncomfortably. His expression was so caustic it made her feel even more selfconscious than she had anticipated. She took a quick mouthful and gulped at the strength of it. It was certainly more potent than what she was used to, and she determined to sip the remaining liquid somewhat more judiciously.

'How about a cigarette to accompany it?' She abruptly found Fraser proffering a packet towards her. 'To save you having to break off again in order to ask for one later,' he taunted in satirical tones.

The stain already covering her cheeks deepened considerably. 'That's very kind of you—thank you.' Rowan still attempted to look innocent as she took one, even if she didn't feel it.

After lighting it for her, Fraser applied a flame to his own and then returned to the bar, but only, it seemed, so that he might collect his drink, for he immediately retraced his steps and settled himself into a chair directly facing her. Much to Rowan's dismay!

'So . . . you were saying?' he prompted inexorably.

'Oh, yes,' she nodded slowly, had another drink from her glass and a leisurely puff or two on her cigarette. 'Now where had I got to?'

'You didn't start.'

'No, that's right, I didn't, did I? My throat suddenly felt so dry.' A further time-consuming sampling of her drink. 'I wonder if I'm coming down with something,' she went on musingly. 'Are you sure you don't find it somewhat on the hot side tonight?'

'No, but I know someone who'll be finding it a damned sight hotter if they don't soon get to the point!' he bit out impatiently.

Rowan grimaced inwardly at his tone but judged it wiser not to antagonise him further with her stalling tactics. 'The point is . . .' she began earnestly, a winsome smile curving her soft lips, 'as we'll be leaving in the morning, and—and we don't like to be on bad terms with anyone if we can avoid it, I thought it might be appropriate if I came to—came to apologise for any inconvenience our barbecues may have caused you. I know you took exception,' understatement! 'to the last one, in particular, but we really thought we were doing the right thing by having them away from the main beach area,' she concluded half vindicatingly, half defiantly.

'Because you considered there was less chance along here of some of your number being picked up as drunk and disorderly?' Fraser charged sarcastically, and not looking at all impressed by her apology.

'Not that I know of, no!' she was quick to deny. 'In any event, there were only a couple who may have had a little too much to drink.'

'But whom you righteously defended at the time, as I recall!'

'Because you made such a commotion about it!'

His mouth set into a hard line. 'You don't think I was entitled to on having my privacy invaded by a pack of well-oiled rowdies?'

'It wasn't intentional,' Rowan defended, if a little awkwardly, knowing he wasn't altogether wrong. 'We were only having a bit of fun, and it's not as if there was any harm done.'

'No doubt only because I happened to be here at the time!' he immediately retorted.

'That's not true!' Her protest was hotly made. 'You have absolutely no basis for assuming anything of the sort.'

'Except an obviously far less naïve approach to life than yours.' His eyes flicked over her satirically and he raised a seemingly amused brow. 'How old did you say you were, honey?'

'I didn't!' she flared, bridling at his superior attitude, and took a larger drink than she intended. It left her feeling a little lightheaded and, as a result, her following words were nowhere near as forceful. 'But as it so happens, I'm twenty. Quite old enough to know my way around, I can assure you.'

'Mmm, I can imagine.'

Rowan glanced at him suspiciously. She wasn't too sure just how she ought to take that. Was he once again implying that she was too young to know what she was talking about, or conversely, implying that, in some matters, he believed she was too experienced for her age?

'Meaning?' Her head lifted to a challenging angle.

He shrugged offhandedly. 'Nothing you don't already know.' Which, to Rowan's mind, was as enigmatic as his last statement had been. 'But now, if that's all you came for . . .' Stubbing out his cigarette, he put his hands on the arms of his chair and rose lithely to his feet.

As she extinguished her own cigarette, Rowan's heart sank to see by her watch that only a quarter of an hour had elapsed since she had entered the beach house. Oh, hell! she despaired, what was she supposed to say now in order to delay him? He was clearly expecting her to make a move towards leaving, but if she didn't keep him a while longer Tanya and Evan would have had hardly any time alone together. With grudging resignation she took another, she hoped, bracing sip from her glass and eyed Fraser provocatively above its rim.

'What makes you think that's the only reason I came?' she asked in a much deeper than normal, and unconsciously seductive, voice.

Fraser's eyes immediately narrowed watchfully. 'Meaning?' it was his turn now to query.

'You're a very attractive man,' she all but mumbled in her selfconsciousness—this really wasn't her style at all—and keeping her gaze fixed to her fingers as they studiously smoothed the material of her dress over her knee.

An inescapable hand beneath her chin suddenly forced her head up. 'Just what are you trying to say, honey?' came the peremptory demand which had her shifting nervously.

'O-only that in these days of the liberated female, it's quite acceptable for a girl to tell a man she'd like to get to know him better,' she returned valiantly.

'I see.' An ironic smile pulled at his lips. Then, straightening, he released her and walked to the bar where he proceeded to refill his glass. 'And this desire to know me better suddenly came upon you this evening, did it?'

'I could have been harbouring it for some time, for all you know,' she offered evasively in lieu of answering.

Fraser drained half the liquid in his glass in one mouthful. 'You certainly hide your feelings very well, then,' he mocked.

'Maybe I was just bashful about declaring them.' Rowan lowered the contents of her own glass a little less rapidly.

'So why should tonight be any different?'

She hunched a honey-coloured shoulder in assumed nonchalance. 'I guess, because we're due to leave in the morning.'

'And just how much better were you planning for us to get to know each other in one night, hmm?' he drawled, a certain—amused?—light in his eyes making her feel even more uncomfortable. 'A little, a lot . . . *the* lot?'

In view of her suspicions, Rowan avoided giving a definite reply. 'I—well—I hadn't thought that far ahead, actually,' she prevaricated, if a little hesitantly, and finished the remains of her drink with as much aplomb as she could manage.

'Perhaps you should have done.' Leaving his glass on the bar, Fraser began walking towards her with a slow, measured stride.

Suddenly all Rowan's feigned composure fled, to be replaced by a feeling of mounting apprehension racing through her at his approach. Having created the situation she was now at something of a loss as to just what she should say, or do, next in order to both retain his attention and yet, simultaneously, keep him at a distance. One thing she did know, however. It was impossible for her to remain passively seated and, hurriedly placing her empty glass on the low coffee table in front of her, she rose to her feet in a carefully casual movement—or at least, that was how she hoped it appeared—and deliberately putting the sofa between them, made for the doors leading on to the verandah.

Not that it brought more than a brief moment's respite from her predicament, for she immediately sensed Fraser had followed her outside, and casting about swiftly for something to distract him—from what, she wasn't quite sure—she moved across to lean her hands on the wooden railing surrounding the verandah and stood gazing out at the first visible line of white, foaming breakers.

'The sea's beautiful in the moonlight, isn't it?' she

commented tightly, trivially, when nothing better came to mind.

Coming to stand beside her, and bringing to the fore again her perturbing awareness of his virile presence, Fraser cupped her cheek in the palm of his hand and resolutely turned her face towards him. 'So are you,' he declared softly, but with a particular inflection in his voice that had all her previous suspicions promptly re-surfacing.

Was she providing him with some amusement? And if so, why? Because he preferred to do the chasing when it came to members of the opposite sex, or because the underlying apprehension in her un-practised attempts to attract him was so apparent? The humiliating thought that it might be the latter, gave her the resolve to return his gaze pertly.

'But not by daylight?' she quipped. To her dismay, though, the words didn't quite come out on the flippant note she had intended. In fact, they sounded distinctly more flirtatious than facetious and, as a result, she berated herself for having finished that gin. She could still feel its effects and it wasn't helping her self-control in the slightest.

'At any time,' he averred in a murmur, and bending his head, had taken possession of her lips before she could even think of evading him.

For a moment Rowan accepted the stimulating pressure of his mouth acquiescently. She knew, of course, that actual resistance was out of the question, for Tanya's sake, but she was also aware that for the same reason she should at least give some response. With this in mind, she allowed Fraser's encircling arms to draw her closer to his solid form as she linked her hands loosely about his lithe waist and her lips parted invitingly beneath the warm domination of his.

In the background she could hear the muted boom of the surf as it tumbled on to the golden shore, but as the minutes passed and Fraser's drugging kisses deepened, she suddenly began to realise, disquietingly, that her heart was beating no less heavily against her ribs than the sea against the sand, and the response he was eliciting with such consummate ease wasn't on her friend's behalf at all—it was purely on her own!

Desperately, Rowan now attempted to apply a brake to her strangely runaway emotions, to regain at least some semblance of control, but found it was an impossible task. Somehow it seemed Fraser had managed to touch a receptive chord somewhere within her and in so doing unleashed a storm of desire it had never before occurred to her she might be capable of feeling.

With her senses spinning helplessly she unknowingly pressed closer against him, her long graceful neck arching rapturously as his lips burnt a fiery, sensuous path to the pulsing base of her throat and his hands moved caressingly upwards from her slender curving hips to her smooth-skinned shoulders. In a continuation of the same unhurried movement, Fraser had slipped the fragile straps of her dress down her arms before Rowan was even conscious of his action, but the touch of his long fingers as they explored the swelling contours of her naked breasts had her sucking in a shocked and shaky breath as she compulsively pulled away.

Fraser made no attempt to prevent her withdrawal, but merely leant back against the railing with his bronzed arms folded across his chest and watched her embarrassed rearrangement of her clothing with an expression on his face that Rowan could only have described as cynical. She also noted, with no little mortification, that his breathing was nowhere near as shallow and unsteady as hers was.

'I hope your friend is properly appreciative of the lengths you're prepared to go to on her behalf,' he remarked sardonically at last.

Rowan flushed guiltily but refused to commit herself. 'I don't know what you're talking about,' she evaded on a low, constricted note.

'You mean, your presence here tonight hasn't just been in order to keep me occupied while Evan and your friend get together?' Grey eyes locked tauntingly with demoralised brown ones.

So he'd guessed that all along, had he? No wonder she'd thought he seemed amused, she reflected dismally. He had just been playing her at her own game! But, unlike her, he obviously hadn't been affected in the slightest by the encounter. The discomfiting knowledge had her struggling furiously to camouflage her loss of composure with an air of unconcern.

'Then, if that was my intention, it would appear I've been successful, wouldn't it?' she countered, and not without a hint of triumph in her tone. After all, it was her only victory of the evening, because Tanya's requested time period would shortly be fulfilled.

'Except for one small detail.' Fraser's patent indifference to her claim had her eyeing him with a wary frown.

'And that is?'

'I'd already decided not to prevent Evan seeing your friend tonight,' he relayed with ironic humour. 'Since the two of you will be leaving tomorrow, I figured there wasn't much point to it.' He uttered a short but extremely aggravating laugh. 'Why else do you think I told him to go on without me when you arrived?'

Recalling her initial surprise at his suggestion at the time, Rowan could only now wish she had given it more thought. But since she hadn't, she determined the outcome wasn't going to be all his way. She would give him something to think about, and his increasingly intolerable self-confidence a shake, somehow!

'Very clever,' she conceded, but with her lips assuming a decidedly mocking curve. 'Although, only so far as it goes, of course.'

'Which means?' She had the pleasure of seeing his eyes narrow attentively.

'You'll find out ... all in good time.' Her accompanying smile was purposely annoying.

Fraser moved so swiftly there wasn't even time for her to take a backward step before a steely grip had ensnared her wrist. 'I'll find out *now*, thanks!' he grated roughly.

'Not from me, you won't!' Rowan defied angrily, trying to prise herself loose.

His fingers tightened painfully. 'Oh yes, I will! Because you won't be leaving here until I do.'

'That's what you think!' she blazed, and raked her nails down the length of his forearm, leaving lines of dark red, swelling welts to mark their passage.

'You little bitch!' Momentarily, Rowan thought he meant to strike her in retaliation and flinched automatically to see his free hand move, but when it imprisoned the hand that had done the damage instead, her relief was promptly tempered with a feeling of disadvantage. 'You might well expect repayment in kind!' he remarked on her involuntary movement derisively as he pulled her against him in order to pin her hands behind her back with only one of his own, then spanned her jaw in a not very gentle clasp. 'But fortunately there's other ways to deal with the likes of you, isn't there, honey?' he suddenly smiled jeeringly into her stormy face.

'Such as?' she dared to challenge, even as she twisted furiously in an effort to break out of the hold that was making her only too conscious of the lean, hard length of him.

In complete control, and denying her liberty with a rankling ease, Fraser waited for her futile attempts to cease before countering sardonically, 'Are you going to tell me what I want to know?'

'No, I'm not!' Her refusal was thrown back defiantly.

With an unexpected shrug, Fraser removed his hand from her chin and calmly proceeded to edge one of her dress straps from her shoulder. 'No?' He arched a goading brow.

A gasp caught in Rowan's throat as the extreme vulnerability of her position was abruptly brought home to her. 'You—you bastard!' she choked helplessly as she felt the thin piece of material sliding inexorably downwards. The rest of her top followed as relentlessly, but only so far as their nearness would allow, when it came to a halt just covering the rosy tip of her quivering breast.

'Well?' He drew a tantalising line along the edge of the precariously placed cloth with his forefinger.

Unable to even struggle now in case she lost what little protection she did have left from his gaze, she had no option but to comply—with a glare. 'There's a possibility we may not be leaving in the morning, after all,' she disclosed reluctantly.

Fraser stiffened. 'But Evan told me your employment at the hotel finished tonight.'

'There's always other jobs.' She went to shrug, then prudently decided against it.

'Not around here—for you two—there won't be.'

'And how can you be so sure of that?' Just because she knew much the same herself, it didn't make her any more resigned to hearing him say it. And especially not in that arrogant manner!

'Because I shall make certain there aren't,' he advised with cool assurance.

Since she was already aware that the Delaney name was an old and valued one in the district, Rowan didn't doubt he could do as he threatened, but at the same time the knowledge didn't sit easily with her either. 'How nice to be so all-powerful!' she gibed acidly. 'I bet it just makes your day to be able to impose your will on somebody who hasn't your advantages!'

'When they happen to be of your kind, you're so right!' Fraser was perfectly willing to agree, mockery paramount.

It wasn't the first time he'd made such a disparaging remark and her temperature rose along with her resentment. 'And just what kind are you trying to suggest that is?' she demanded—then had her attention diverted by the further movement of her top as she unconsciously strained away from him, and flushed hotly to see the last of the screening material slowly but surely falling. 'All right, so you've had your fun at my expense, now let me go!' she cried distractedly, aching with embarrassment, and beginning to fight against his confining hold once again. There was no reason not to now.

'Uh-uh,' he vetoed laconically. 'You scratch, remember?'

Rowan shook her head wildly, her long blonde hair swirling about her shoulders. 'And is that why you . . .?' She came to a shuddering stop, her breathing ragged. Why he'd done it really wasn't the most important aspect right now. 'Oh, please!' she begged anguishedly. Just having to plead with him made it doubly painful. 'I'm sorry for scratching you, but please let me go.'

His firmly moulded mouth shaped ironically. 'You're embarrassed?' he queried in mildly amused surprise as, even if he didn't actually release her, he did at least right her state of undress. Although entirely at his leisure, she noted infuriatedly.

'Wasn't I supposed to be?' she retorted promptly in pungent accents.

'After the way you come on when you're kissed, honey, who could say?'

'Oh!' Rowan felt her face burn with selfconscious colour again. That damned gin! she cursed silently. She'd never touch the stuff again. 'Well, now—now you know, don't you?'

Fraser inclined his dark head wryly in acknowledgment. 'And can I also be certain you'll be leaving tomorrow?'

'Why? Is that a condition for your releasing me?' Her eyes widened sarcastically.

In return his own gaze swept pointedly over her vainly squirming form. 'It would appear that way,' he drawled lazily.

'Because you're suddenly doubtful the great Delaney name will be sufficient to bar us from getting work in the area?'

'Not at all,' he refuted her gibe with an untroubled hunching of one broad shoulder. 'Apart from the fact that I know there's very few positions available at present, anyway, those that are vacant are all with friends, and . . .' he paused to cast her a taunting smile, 'we're a very close-knit community here at the Bay.'

Suddenly, and to her chagrin, now that those mortifying moments were behind her Rowan annoyingly found her wayward senses responding to that attractive curving of his lips, even as her awareness of his rugged physique perturbingly returned. All too well could she feel through the gossamery cotton of her dress the muscular length of his thighs as they pressed against hers, the thrust of his lean hips emphasised by the close grip he had on her hands as he kept them pinned to the small of her back, the powerful build of his chest as it brushed the swelling mounds of her breasts, and in an effort to overcome such awareness she determinedly channelled her thoughts into one emotion—indignation—due to both his attitude and his intentions.

'Then, if that's the case, I wouldn't have thought any assurance from me was necessary!' she eventually replied to his last irritatingly confident remark with a derisive expression.

'In that regard, it's probably not,' he conceded chaffingly. 'But having experienced for myself the way in which you attempt to attain your own ends, I just figured it might save someone else having to suffer the same.'

To save someone else suffering the same! If there had been any suffering, it had all been on her part, not his!

'How incredibly altruistic of you!' Rowan applauded satirically, her breathing deepening uncontrollably with the force of her escalating anger. How dared he imply that this evening's attempted ruse was a common practice on her part! 'Unfortunately, though, I can't guarantee anything of the kind. You see, Tanya and I make our decisions *together*, not separately. So now what are you going to do?' She allowed herself the satisfaction of giving him a provoking smile. 'Refuse to let go of me until you've managed to browbeat Tanya into promising to leave?'

His steel grey eyes surveyed her indolently. 'While continuing to amuse myself at your expense in the meantime?' he taunted.

Rowan swallowed nervously, her smile fading as rapidly as it had come. 'You w-wouldn't dare,' she faltered rather than denounced, as she had intended.

'Correction . . . I don't care to.' In an abrupt change of manner his expression became scornfully dismissing as, to her surprise, but nonetheless heartfelt relief, he at last turned her loose. 'And since your little charade has already made me late . . .' looking significantly at his watch.

With a somewhat bewildered frown drawing her winged brows together, Rowan massaged her reddened wrists absently. Of course she was thankful to have been released, and yet. . . . That surely wasn't pique she felt because he was so obviously able to brush her aside without a second thought, when she suspected it would be impossible for her to do the same to him? The analysis was too disturbing to contemplate further and, with a clearing shake of her head, she lifted her chin fractionally higher.

'Yes—well, I'll say goodnight, and perhaps goodbye, then,' she retorted flippantly, making for the steps. 'With luck, we won't see each other again.'

'I'll keep my fingers crossed.' The drawl was back in Fraser's voice as he concurred mockingly with her sentiments.

Stopping in order to remove her sandals before she reached the sand, Rowan steadfastly refused to answer or even acknowledge the goading remark. But as she stormed along the beach a few seconds later it was with the disgruntled mutter of, 'No more than I will, believe me!' on her lips.

From her standpoint the evening had been a débâcle from beginning to end, and any subsequent contact with Fraser Delaney could only serve to remind her of a humiliating experience she would much rather forget!

CHAPTER TWO

SLEEP was a long time coming to Rowan when she returned to the small room she shared with Tanya at the hotel, and no sooner had she finally managed to doze off than she was almost immediately re-awakened by her friend's arrival. And one look at Tanya's starry-eyed countenance was enough to confirm her worst fears.

'Evan's asked you not to leave,' she deduced with a groan.

Tanya nodded vigorously, her pleasantly rounded face wreathed in smiles, and completely unaware that her companion's groan hadn't been caused by her still sleepy state. 'Not only that, but he's found us jobs as well!' she relayed excitedly as she crossed the room and sank down on to the end of Rowan's bed. 'I've had a fantastic evening, thanks to you.' She gave Rowan a playful push on the leg. 'See, I told you you could do it, didn't I?'

Pushing herself into a sitting position, Rowan rested her chin on her updrawn knees. 'Oh, I did it all right,' she granted wryly.

Her friend picked up the ruefulness in her tone immediately. 'Well, you did, didn't you?' she half laughed, half frowned. 'I mean, we didn't see Fraser all night, so we presumed you must have been successful.'

If time was to be the only criterion then Rowan supposed she could claim to have been triumphant. 'Yes—well, in that regard, I guess I was,' she shrugged. Then, with a falsely bright smile, went on swiftly, 'But don't let's talk about me.' That, she definitely wanted to avoid! 'I'm more interested in hearing what Evan had to say. And especially those jobs you reckon he's found us.'

Tanya was only too ready to tell her. 'He says we can work for him,' she divulged elatedly.

'Work for him!' Rowan's astonishment was evident in her widening eyes. 'Doing what?'

'Working in the nut processing factory.'

'The *Delaneys'* factory?'

'Mmm, that's right,' Tanya confirmed blithely. 'He said they've been considering putting on one, or maybe two, more girls for the last month or so.'

'"They" being he and—and Fraser?' came the drily voiced request for clarification.

On receiving an endorsing nod from her friend, Rowan promptly gave vent to a peal of humourless laughter which brought a look of puzzlement to Tanya's features.

'Why, what's wrong with that?' she queried rather bewilderedly.

'The pair of you must have rocks in your heads if you think Fraser's going to meekly accept our presence at any factory of his, that's what's wrong with it!' Rowan informed her expressively. 'You know very well that until tonight he's done everything he possibly could to keep you and Evan from seeing each other. So what makes you think he's suddenly going to change now and allow you to work together, of all things?'

'Because Evan's solely in charge of the factory, and its staff, that's why,' Tanya explained briefly, her attention obviously on something else. 'But what did you mean, "until tonight" Fraser was trying to keep us apart?'

Rowan hunched away from the question restively, wishing she'd chosen her words with more care. 'Oh, just that I was told Fraser hadn't intended doing anything about you seeing Evan tonight, that's all,' she tried to dismiss the matter as casually as possible.

'Then if he didn't object to my seeing Evan tonight, he won't mind in future either, will he?' Tanya happily jumped to her own conclusion.

'Uh-uh!' Rowan had to ruefully disabuse her. 'That was only because he expected us to be leaving later today.' Midnight had come and gone over an hour ago. 'Otherwise I doubt his stand would have altered in the slightest.'

'Oh!' The other girl's face crumpled dejectedly. 'He actually told you that, did he?'

'Sorry,' Rowan smiled compassionately, nodding.

With a sigh, Tanya attempted to forget her own disappointment for the moment and looked closely at her friend instead. 'But how would that have come into the conversation?' she probed curiously. Then, gasping, 'When you were leaving, you didn't by any chance disclose what you'd done, or anything like that, did you?'

Rowan's lips twisted obliquely. 'No, I didn't disclose what I'd done ... because I didn't do anything! At least, not anything that could be classified as having fooled Fraser Delaney,' she qualified on a self-mocking note. 'Unfortunately, he guessed from the minute I arrived just why I was there.'

'Oh, no!' Tanya's blue eyes became shaded with dismay. 'And I'm so sorry to have put you in such an awkward position. Was he—was he very irate about it?'

'Since it was some time before he kindly let me know I was wasting my time, no, totally and imperviously self-assured is how I would have described him,' Rowan grimaced. 'In fact, the man's an arrogant, overbearing, and callous swine!' Unable to stop now that she'd started, she swept long strands of hair over her shoulder with an impatient hand, and continued hotly, 'He's despotic, implacable, and downright ruthless, and if he ever refers to me in those disdainful accents as *my type*,' she mimicked wrathfully, 'again, so help me, I'll give him a sight more than a couple of scratches on his damned arm to remember me by!'

Tanya stared at her, stunned. 'S-scratches on his arm?' she quizzed weakly as if that was all she'd been able to grasp of the unexpected revelation.

'He wouldn't let go of my wrist, so I—er—retaliated,' Rowan shrugged, trying to make light of it now that her pent-up feelings had finally been released.

'But why did he have hold of your wrist at all?' in the same faint, perplexed voice.

'Because he wanted an assurance from me that we wouldn't stay in the district,' Rowan conveniently concealed more than she revealed.

'He's that set against my seeing Evan?' forlornly.

'He's that set against *both* of us,' came the sardonic correction. 'At a guess, I'd say I'm the one he objects to most.' Or, if she hadn't been before, she probably was now!

'But why?'

'Why me most of all, or why either of us?'

'Either of us,' Tanya elucidated with a frown.

Rowan reached for a cigarette from the packet on the small table between their two beds and, lighting it, expelled the smoke slowly. 'I told you the answer to that on the beach yesterday. Because we don't come from his socially acceptable circle, that's why. The Fraser Delaneys of this world go to the Palm Garden,' referring to the Kurrawa Bay Hotel's tree and shrub-enclosed dining area, 'for their immaculately prepared barbecues, they don't brush sand off their steaks on the beach like we do, you know,' she half laughed ironically. 'Besides, he's probably already got some girl with the proper background all picked out for Evan and he doesn't want you upsetting his plans.'

'Evan's never mentioned anyone, though, and I've certainly never seen him with anybody else,' Tanya commented doubtfully.

'Oh, I didn't say Evan necessarily knew anything about it,' she was hastily reassured. 'Just that Fraser could quite possibly have it in mind. On his five-year plan for future developments, or something similar.'

Tanya digested this in silence for a while and, obviously cheered by the somewhat less depressing explanation, her lips resumed their more customary upward curve. 'Somehow I get the impression the time you spent with Fraser hasn't exactly endeared him to you,' she speculated wryly.

'You mean, it shows?' quipped Rowan in an ironic tone, and drew deeply, steadyingly, on her cigarette.

'Only a little,' Tanya grinned. 'So would you care to tell me just what happened at the beach house this evening?'

'Nothing in particular,' Rowan denied with a shrug. 'It's just his general attitude that sets me burning. He's so damned sure of himself!' Her eyes sought her companion's sympathetically. 'And that's why I'm positive he'll never countenance you and me working for Evan. He's made up his mind we're bad news, and nothing on earth is going to make him change his opinion. I'm sorry, but I really think you're just going to have to reconcile yourself to the fact that we don't have any chance but to move on to new pastures.'

'But if Evan *can* get us work . . .' Tanya held out hopefully.

Not that Rowan supposed he could, but . . . 'Well, even if he did, where are we going to live?' She spread her hands questioningly. 'We can't afford to stay here,' indicating the hotel, 'and even if we could, Kurrawa Bay's too far from the plantation anyway.'

'I know, but Evan's already considered all that.' Tanya could hardly get the words out quickly enough in her desire to pass on the information. 'There's a small village about a kilometre or so from the plantation and we can get accommodation there. Apparently one of the girls who works for them— grafting the young trees, or something like that, I think he said—lives with just her widowed mother in a large old house in this village and, in—in preparation for tonight,' she lowered her eyes shyly, blushing, 'he had a word with them during the week to see if they'd be prepared to take in a couple of boarders.'

'Whereupon they said yes, the extra money would come in very handy,' inserted Rowan drily.

'How did you know?' Tanya gazed at her in amazement.

Her look was returned with a rueful smile. 'It was a foregone conclusion, wasn't it, what with your pleased expression, the widowed mother in the large house, and all?'

'Put like that, I guess so,' Tanya laughed. 'Although it does solve our problem regarding accommodation, doesn't it?'

'Hmm.' Rowan pressed her lips together wryly.

'Now all that needs to be done is for someone to solve our problem concerning Fraser Delaney.'

'And I still think Evan's already done that,' put in her friend stoutly. Then, abruptly, her expression clouded. 'Or is it just that you don't fancy staying in the area any longer?'

Of course she didn't, after tonight's galling episode! Though she could hardly say as much when Tanya's reason for wishing to extend their visit was such a valid one.

'It doesn't matter to me whether we stay or leave,' she alleged with a pseudo-indifferent shake of her head. 'I just don't want you to get your hopes up too high, that's all.' She bit at her lip contritely. 'I know I seem to keep repeating myself, but honestly, there's still no way I can see Fraser agreeing to our employment.' How could she, after the pains he'd gone to in order to convince her otherwise?

'But that's just it, don't you see?' Tanya burst out triumphantly. 'Fraser doesn't *have* to agree to our employment, because Evan's in charge of the factory!'

'And does he also own it?' Rowan's brows peaked enquiringly.

'Well, no, I don't think so. As far as I'm aware, Fraser's the one who actually owns the whole plantation. Why?'

'Because despite Evan being responsible for the factory ... nominally,' with a significant pause, 'I can't imagine Fraser, as the owner, not having the right of veto over any decision he makes.'

It was clear such a consideration hadn't entered Tanya's thoughts, for her shoulders immediately slumped despondently, but only momentarily, and then her demeanour was brightening again as she declared, 'Although that possibility certainly didn't seem to occur to Evan when he suggested we work at the plantation.'

'Maybe because Fraser's never had cause to overrule any of his decisions . . . until now.'

Sighing disconsolately, Tanya rose to her feet and began preparing for bed. 'You're not usually so pessimistic,' she looked back over her shoulder to muse.

'I'm sorry,' Rowan apologised sincerely, her resentment of Fraser Delaney uncontrollably surging to the fore again as she saw her friend's downcast expression. It was all his fault gentle, placid-natured Tanya looked so miserable! 'It's just that . . .'

'I know,' interposed Tanya forlornly. 'You're not anticipating Evan bringing anything but disappointing news with him when he returns in the morning.'

'Later this morning,' Rowan amended with a half smile, attempting to inject a little levity into the situation. 'What time's he supposed to be coming?' If Fraser let him come at all, that was! Although she kept that suspicion well hidden, of course.

'Somewhere between eight-thirty and nine,' she was advised as Tanya headed for the bathroom. 'He was going to drive us out to the Crossroads.'

'Where?' In the act of putting out her cigarette, Rowan looked up to query.

'The Crossroads. That's the name of the village near the plantation.'

Rowan nodded her acknowledgment, and after Tanya had left the room, slid down on to her back once more to lie staring thoughtfully up at the ceiling. She hadn't enjoyed casting such a dark shadow over the other girl's hopes, and the fact that she'd needed to made her seethe with indignation. Why shouldn't Tanya see Evan if she wanted to? Or, come to that, why didn't Evan tell his autocratic cousin where to get off? It was obvious Fraser Delaney needed someone to knock some of that self-assuredness out of him, and if it hadn't been for the fact that she and Tanya were leaving—which she didn't doubt for a minute—Rowan wouldn't have minded taking on the project herself. But this time, on her terms, not under assumed ones on somebody else's behalf!

The two girls—one eagerly hopeful, the other resentful but resigned—were ready and waiting outside the hotel at least fifteen minutes before Evan was due to arrive later that morning, and, sliding on her dark glasses in order to shield her eyes from the glare of the early morning sun on the azure blue sea, Tanya glanced briefly up and down the almost deserted Esplanade.

'Shall we wait here, or across the road?' she asked conversationally of her companion.

'Across the road,' decided Rowan, adjusting the angle of her floppy straw hat rather than resort to sunglasses. 'At least there's a seat over there. We may as well be comfortable while we wait.'

'Okay,' Tanya's agreement was equally given, and carrying their luggage of a single case apiece, they crossed the wide palm-adorned road to the wooden seat overlooking the beach, where they settled down to wait in the shade of a spreading poinciana.

Still there almost three-quarters of an hour later, Rowan reluctantly felt obliged to voice the worst. 'Have you considered the possibility that he may be—er—prevented from coming altogether?' she put forward discomfitedly.

'No, of course not!' Tanya refused to even

contemplate such an idea. 'Besides, he said somewhere between eight-thirty and nine, and there's still a few minutes to go yet.'

With a shrug Rowan went back to viewing those swimmers who were taking advantage of the un-crowded surf, but when another quarter of an hour had elapsed without Evan making an appearance, she couldn't help pointing out, no matter how unwillingly, 'The only bus heading north of Brisbane today leaves in thirty minutes, you know.' Even if Evan did turn up, but with bad news, there was no point in their wasting time and money by staying at Kurrawa Bay for another night.

'I know,' Tanya acceded, sighing. 'It's beginning to look as if you could be right, isn't it? Although I was still hoping . . .' She broke off suddenly, a broad relieved smile rapidly replaced her dejected expression. 'No, there he is! That's him coming now!' she cried excitedly on seeing a bright red Torana approaching along the Esplanade.

The sporty sedan purred to a stop beside them and, alighting quickly, Evan headed towards the two girls with a ruefully apologetic look on his boyishly good-looking face.

'I'm sorry I'm late, but something came up,' he explained hurriedly.

'Something, in the form of your cousin?' surmised Rowan immediately, drily.

'I guess you could say that,' he allowed, lips twisting involuntarily. 'Although everything's settled now. So if you'd like to hop in the car . . .' He bent down to grasp a case in each hand.

Casting her friend an elated, 'I told you so' look, Tanya responded to the remark with a willing smile and swiftly rose to her feet. Rowan, on the other hand, stayed exactly where she was, staring up at him in undisguised amazement.

'Are you trying to tell me Fraser has approved our employment?' she quizzed incredulously.

'Uh-huh,' Evan smiled wryly.

'Good lord!' She shook her head in disbelief. 'Whatever dire persuasions did you have to use to accomplish that?'

'What makes you think I needed to use any?' he countered with a laugh.

She sent him an askance gaze. 'You forget, I spent an extremely enlightening hour or so with your cousin last night. And if that wasn't enough,' her glance turned ironic, 'you as good as confirmed it with your comments a few moments ago.'

'Yes—well, I'm sorry about last night,' he began awkwardly, and had her struggling to stifle a shocked gasp.

'Fraser told you what happened?' she queried in a tight voice.

'That he intended to make certain no one in the area employed you? Yes,' he nodded ruefully, but unwittingly enabling her to breathe a little easier. 'However, I guess he must have had a change of heart overnight,' he continued quickly, 'because I certainly didn't require any dire persuasion,' with a half laugh, 'to bring him round to my way of thinking this morning, I can assure you.'

'But you did need some, I gather,' she persisted shrewdly.

'A little,' he conceded, hunching one shoulder somewhat sheepishly.

Immediately suspicious, Rowan eyed him closely. 'Such as?' she probed.

'Who cares?' broke in Tanya unworriedly. 'We're employed, that's what's important.'

'I'd still like to know.' Rowan refused to be put off and kept her eyes resolutely on Evan. She didn't trust Fraser Delaney one little bit, and if something had made him amenable to Evan's suggestion, then it sure hadn't been because of a change of heart. Of that she was only too positive!

'It was nothing cataclysmic, believe me,' Evan smiled encouragingly. 'Just a guarantee on my part that if either of you proved unsatisfactory, then you would both agree to resign. And since I couldn't see that happening, I naturally accepted the condition on your behalf.'

It didn't sound unreasonable, and yet she was still wary. 'So you'll still be our employer, then?' she queried speculatively.

'Oh, yes,' he nodded. 'You'll both be working for me.'

Rowan shook her head quickly. 'That wasn't what I asked.'

For a moment Evan stared at her uncomprehendingly, then suddenly realising, part laughed, part frowned, 'But everyone on the plantation is employed by Fraser . . . even me.'

'But I thought Tanya said *you* employed all those who worked in the factory.'

'Well, so I do. In the same way a personnel manager employs people in a large company, but that doesn't personally make him their employer. In any case,' he paused to give her a slightly baffled look, 'I can't really see why you should feel so worried about it. Fraser doesn't interfere with my running of the plant, and the only female staff he usually comes in contact with, apart from his housekeeper, of course, are his secretary and the two girls who work in the seedling and grafting sections.'

Having stood by patiently, Tanya now broke in to urge, 'Oh, come on, Rowan, stop looking for pitfalls where there are none. As I said, the main thing is that we've got somewhere to work, not who's actually our legal employer.'

'I suppose you're right,' Rowan gave in with a sigh, allowing herself to be persuaded, and rising to her feet at last. She still didn't like it, but as it obviously meant so much to her friend she supposed the least she could do was to give it a try.

At the same time, however, she couldn't help but remember the strength of Fraser's opposition to their presence to date, and as they made their way across to Evan's car she just had to make her troublesome thoughts known.

'Doesn't it seem strange to you, though, that your cousin should have had such an abrupt change of mind?' she asked him speculatively. 'I mean, up until now he's done all he possibly could to stop you seeing Tanya at all, so that's made him become this co-operative all of a sudden?'

With a fond look for the brown-haired girl on his other side, Evan shrugged unconcernedly. 'Maybe he's just realised we're serious about our relationship.'

'You didn't ask him why?' Her brows lifted in surprise.

He loaded their cases into the luggage compartment and then held the rear door open for her. 'I wasn't particularly interested in his reasons, only the result of them,' his reply was casually made as she moved past him to slide on to the smoothly upholstered seat.

Frowning, Rowan watched him close her door and then usher Tanya into the front of the car. If she'd been in his shoes she knew for a certainty that she would definitely have wanted to know the reasons governing Fraser's attitude! Although, come to that, if she had been in Evan's place, she wouldn't have permitted Fraser to dictate the terms of her love life in the first place, she decided firmly.

As the man in her thoughts took his place behind the wheel and the car started to move, Rowan's inward contemplations continued. So why hadn't he protested at the interference? she wondered. Because Fraser, cousin or not, was still his employer, after all? Or because ... She hesitated, unwilling to even ponder over the surmise that was springing to mind, then pushed on determinedly. Or because Evan either hadn't cared enough to protest, or else didn't have the guts to stand up for himself? Of course she could be wrong on both counts, she hurriedly attempted to give him the benefit of the doubt, and certainly neither of them augured very well for Tanya, but what other reason could there be when he'd only just made it patently clear that he was prepared to accept Fraser's arbitrary and capricious decrees without question?

'So what will we be doing at the factory?' Tanya's eagerly questioning voice interrupted Rowan's reverie and fortunately gave her something else to concentrate on as she listened for Evan's reply.

'Nothing very glamorous, I'm afraid,' he smiled briefly, ruefully, at the girl beside him. 'Just checking the nuts on the sorting conveyors before they're packed, mainly.'

'Checking for what?' she asked interestedly.

'Any discoloration, parts of shells the separating machine may have missed, high ridges around the centre of the nuts that signify they're the ones that would have germinated.'

'Don't they all?' Tanya flicked him an amazed glance. 'Germinate, if left, I mean.'

'Uh-uh.' He shook his head in negation. 'Only a certain percentage will ever take root. It's nature's way of controlling the species, I guess.'

'Why do they need to be sorted, though?' Rowan now leant forward to enter the conversation. 'It's too late to do anything with them by then, isn't it?'

'With regard to planting? Oh, yes,' he confirmed. 'Even if we did use the harvested nuts to provide rooting stock, which we don't. We keep special seedling trees for that purpose and theirs are the nuts we plant. None of their crop ever goes into the factory. No, the reason we remove those that were intended to germinate is that they not only look slightly different to the others, but they also taste different as well.'

'Not as nice?' deduced Tanya.

'Not quite as nice,' he endorsed wryly.

Rowan leant back in her seat again, her curiosity appeased for the moment now that she knew the type of work they would be undertaking, and stubbornly resisted displaying any further interest in the plantation or its management. Since the mere thought of its owner was sufficient to have her smouldering resentfully, it felt as if she was betraying herself in some way to show an interest in Fraser's means of livelihood, so she ignored the desultory conversation being continued in the front of the vehicle and absently surveyed the countryside they were passing through instead.

At the moment they were travelling between the last of the luxuriant green fields of soon-to-be-harvested sugarcane that surrounded Kurrawa Bay, but presently they turned off the main highway and began leaving the coastal plains behind them as the road they were now following meandered between the hills and valleys of an increasingly undulating landscape.

From one of the tourist brochures available at the hotel, Rowan had learned that this whole area had originally been part of the 'Big Scrub', as it had been known a century and more ago. An immense rain forest covering many thousands of hectares, its dense vegetation had been found to contain vast numbers of cedar and other rare trees, including the macadamia— or Queensland bush nut, to give it its popular name— but unfortunately, once it was discovered, the cedar-getters of the time hadn't taken long to deplete its supply of the red gold so that, nowadays, only less accessible pockets of the rain forest remained, while the rest of the land had gradually been cleared for grazing and the growing of tropical fruits.

It was still beautiful country, though, Rowan had to admit, with its rich red, volcanic earth, rolling hills dressed in mantles of tall green grass, and clumps of darker canopied trees lining every glinting creek and gully. Because they had no transport of their own, it was the farthest inland Tanya and herself had been since arriving at the Bay, and she was finding the journey to be not only more interesting than she had anticipated, but the restful scenery a pleasant change as well.

'What do you think, Rowan?'

Brought out of her silent contemplation of an avocado plantation they were just passing by the sound of her friend's questioning voice, Rowan turned away from the window with a start. 'I'm sorry, I wasn't listening to what you were saying. What do I think about what?' she frowned her request for elucidation.

'Evan was just asking if we'd like to have a look over the plantation, or if we'd prefer to go straight to Mrs Raymond's,' Tanya explained over her shoulder.

'Mrs Raymond's?' The furrows across Rowan's forehead became even deeper.

Tanya's eyes rolled expressively skywards. 'The lady we'll be boarding with, of course! Haven't you heard *anything* we've been saying?'

'Sorry,' Rowan apologised ruefully for her lack of attention. 'Why, are we nearly there?'

'Not really, apparently there's still a way to go yet. Evan thought we might like to see over the place before we start work there, that's all.'

Momentarily, Rowan was inclined to ask whether Fraser was likely to be there too before giving her answer, but on further consideration she decided that was extremely unlikely unless he'd departed even earlier than they had. A circumstance she didn't think probable since he was, according to previous information from Evan, supposedly taking a well-earned vacation for a few weeks.

'I don't mind,' she now shrugged negligently. 'If that's what you want to do, it's okay by me.' Provided she didn't have to suffer Fraser's highhanded presence, she didn't mind where they went.

'Oh, good,' Tanya smiled at her. 'Because I thought it sounded like a great idea. At least then it won't seem so strange when we start work tomorrow—never having done anything like this before.'

'Is that when we start ... tomorrow?' Rowan's return glance was wryly humorous. Apparently there were a number of subjects she'd missed hearing them discuss.

'I thought we might as well,' Tanya nodded. 'Especially since Evan will be here to give us any hints and tips we may need.'

'Oh, so you don't intend returning immediately to the beach house, then, Evan?' Rowan sat forward once more in order to speak directly to him.

'No, I thought I'd stick around, at least for a while,' he swung his head briefly to grin.

'I can't for the life of me think why,' she teased, adopting a pondering pose.

A remark which had Tanya colouring selfconsciously as she responded with a mock-threatening gaze before hoping to forestall any further comments of a similarly bantering nature by pointing to a steeply sloping hillside on their right covered with orderly rows of palm-like plants and asking swiftly, 'Are they bananas over there?'

'Mmm,' confirmed Evan on a dry note, guessing her question had been made out of defensiveness rather than ignorance. 'They grow them on slopes like that because . . .'

'Don't you dare say, because that's how they get the bend in them,' interrupted Rowan wryly in case he intended following with the age-old joke.

'I wasn't going to,' he denied, laughing. 'I was going to say, they're grown on those steep slopes because, like macadamias, they require good draining due to their strong aversion to wet feet.'

'You mean, your plantation is on a sharp hill like that too?' Tanya gasped.

'Oh, no, macadamias aren't quite as temperamental in that regard as bananas . . . thank heavens,' Evan explained with feeling. 'They're satisfied with nice gentle gradients.'

'Considering they're a native of the rain forest, though, I would have thought they'd like a lot of water,' surmised Rowan.

'They do,' he agreed, ironically. 'But they dislike it sitting around even more.'

'Oh, I see,' she half laughed whimsically and, as the

minutes passed, returned to her contemplation of the view outside.

Shortly, the landscape began levelling out a little more and after rounding a sweeping bend in the road they could see a small village clustered about a wide intersection just ahead of them.

'The Crossroads,' Evan informed them as he started to slow and prepared to make a right-hand turn at the junction. 'And that's the Raymonds' house, where you'll be staying.' He pointed out a large, bougain-villea-bedecked house on the outskirts as they passed.

It looked a pleasant enough place, as did the village itself, judging by what she had been able to see of either of them, Rowan conceded. Even if it wasn't exactly a hub of activity, she couldn't help adding irrepressibly, because apart from the few dozen houses, there didn't appear to be anything else there except an old wooden church, a small general store, and a somewhat rundown garage. There wasn't even a pub, which was usually the first enterprise to follow any more of the population into the bush!

'Home sweet home,' Evan broke the silence with a grin only a short time later as he turned in through a wide gateway and indicated the house situated on the top of the rise before them.

With two magnificent pencil pines standing guard on either side of the front steps, and encircled by well-kept lawns and flowering trees, it was a very impressive building even from a distance—and just the type of house she would have expected Fraser to own, grimaced Rowan acidly. Large and obviously com-modious, it completely dominated the surrounding area, and although its white-painted, two-storeyed colonial design—complete with iron lace-enclosed balconies and porches—indicated its age, it was just as apparent that no expense had been spared to retain it in such outstanding condition.

About fifty metres or so to the right, and connected to the house by a covered walkway, was a much more modern, hexagonal-shaped building constructed of natural stained timbers, which Evan pointed out was the office, and as they continued on past both, accompanied the information with the advice, 'I'll show you over that on the way back, after you've seen the factory.'

Following the contour of the slight hill down the other side, it was possible to see the plantation set out before them now with the plastic-domed nursery and grafting sections on their left, and row upon row of trees stretching out in every direction so that it seemed as if there wasn't a hill within sight that wasn't covered with them.

'Good lord, I had no idea the place would be this large!' Tanya exclaimed involuntarily, and unknowingly putting Rowan's own grudging thoughts into words. 'There must be millions of trees out there.'

'Not quite.' Evan shook his head in humorous denial. 'Only about eighty thousand, actually.'

'Oh, hardly enough to worry about,' was the joking retort. Then, with blue eyes widening in astonishment to see a streamlined coach suddenly approaching them, 'What on earth's that doing here?'

'Tourists,' he explained with a laugh, and reciprocated the coach driver's wave as they passed. 'They like to have a look over the plantation, see how the nuts are processed, and maybe buy some from the shop.'

'And where is the shop? At the factory?' inserted Rowan. It seemed the most logical place for it.

'That's right,' Evan confirmed her reasoning. 'We sell the whole range of nuts; loose, packaged, salted, chocolate-covered, you name it; as well as a small range of cosmetics.'

'Cosmetics!' she repeated with an incredulous laugh. 'That's a ring-in, isn't it?'

'Only in the fact that they're not meant to be eaten,' he grinned. 'But otherwise, I'll have you know, macadamia oil-based preparations are extremely good for the skin.'

'Oh, you've used them yourself, have you?' she queried facetiously.

Evan aimed a swatting hand at her across the back of the seat, but which she laughingly evaded with ease. 'No, I haven't used them myself. I've just read the pamphlets that come with them,' he relayed drily.

'They're not also made on the property, then?' It was Tanya who had a question to ask this time.

'No, we provide the nuts for the oil, but the products are made elsewhere.'

Moments later the factory, with a sign denoting *Delaney Plantations* emblazoned across the front, came into sight and Evan was soon bringing the car to a halt in the car park beside the compact, steel building. Opening her own door, Rowan stepped out mechanically, her eyes surveying the structure speculatively as she wondered just what she was doing there. She was already filled with misgivings about working for Fraser Delaney, and she hadn't even been inside the plant yet!

CHAPTER THREE

A WEEK later and Rowan was once again looking round the factory, but on this occasion from the doorway which connected it with the shop where she had just finished serving another busload of visitors. It wasn't anyone in particular's job to serve in the shop, the girls working on the sorting conveyors took it in turns mostly, but it provided a nice break every once in a while from the repetitiveness of the work and a chance to escape from the noise of the machinery, for although they all wore ear-muffs to protect their hearing, the sound of the shelling machine as it cracked the iron-hard covering of the macadamia was still quite noticeable.

Now, as she readjusted the concealing cap they were required to wear over their hair and replaced her ear-muffs and rubber gloves before returning inside, Rowan suddenly heard another vehicle pull up outside and saw that it was Fraser in one of the plantation's two Jackaroo four-wheel-drives. Clad in denims and a faded red and grey check shirt, he strode quickly past the shop doors—on his way to see Evan who was at the moment talking to one of the drivers who had just brought in more bins laden with the tasty crop, she supposed.

The sight of him had her pulling a rueful face and remembering those few times she'd come in contact with him during the last seven days. His attitude had been one of such cool arrogance that she'd longed to cut him down to size with some scathing retort, but as

she very well knew—if only for her friend's sake, once
again—that would have been extremely unwise, not to
mention suicidal, and in the end she had just had to
grit her teeth and pretend as best she could to be
completely unaffected by his presence. Even so, she
guessed that was still better than having him
continually attempting to find reasons for dismissing
them, as she had half expected him to do, although she
still couldn't quite rid herself of the feeling that he was
only biding his time before voicing an objection Evan
wouldn't be capable of overcoming. It was a
dispiriting thought, as well as a somewhat nerve-
racking one, and with a grimace she about-turned and
re-entered the factory before she gave him the
opportunity to accuse her of loitering, or something
similar!

Back at her place once more, Rowan had only just
begun sorting again when both Evan and Fraser
entered by a side door and came walking across the
floor towards where Tanya and herself were working.
A surreptitious glance from beneath the cover of long,
glossy lashes showed Evan to be beckoning to Tanya
to join them, but the slight crease which had begun to
mark Rowan's wide brow as a result of his action
immediately deepened to one of wary presentiment
when he promptly gestured for her to do the same.

So what nefarious plan had Fraser's tortuous mind
managed to come up with now? she puzzled
suspiciously, never doubting for one minute that he
wasn't the instigator of this little meeting. The
distinctly mocking light she had observed in the
metallic grey depths of his eyes as they had locked
momentarily with hers had been sufficient to convince
her of that!

Within the quieter precincts of the shop both girls

removed their ear-muffs, and it was obvious from the perplexed look on her face that Tanya was no wiser regarding the reason for their having been singled out than Rowan was. But whereas Rowan was apprehensively aware of Fraser leaning indolently against the counter, Tanya only seemed confused as her gaze sought Evan's quizzically and she waited for him to speak.

'Yes, well, I'm sorry, but it seems we have something of a problem up at the house,' he began, rather nervously to Rowan's ears, and including them both in a rueful glance. 'You know Alice—Alice Earnshaw—our housekeeper, of course. Well, Fraser tells me she fell and broke her leg a couple of hours ago. They've only just arrived back from having it set.'

Naturally, Rowan was only too willing to add her condolences to those Tanya was making. Fraser's goodnatured housekeeper had the happy knack of being able to get on well with everyone. But it also raised a point she felt needed to be clarified, and she phrased it tautly.

'So how does that involve us?'

Evan half smiled diffidently, although there was nothing whatsoever even remotely resembling deprecation in Fraser's stance, she noticed. 'Well, we'd like one of you to take over from her—or at least, give her some assistance,' he amended swiftly, 'until she recovers.'

So she was right! Rowan fumed inwardly. Fraser had merely been biding his time . . . the conniving rat! And if they refused, what then? Would that be construed as their work having proved unsatisfactory, and they'd be expected to leave?

'Why one of us?' she disregarded Evan in order to demand of the taller man. After all, he was the source of all their problems, wasn't he? 'Why not one of the other girls who've been here longer?'

'Because from what I've seen, it's apparent there's just one too many of you doing the sorting, and since you two were the last employed . . .' He hunched one broad shoulder explicitly.

Unfortunately, it wasn't a statement Rowan could contradict, for it was a thought that had often occurred to her too during the last week. There *wasn't* really enough work for all of them, and more often than not they ended by getting in each other's way.

'In other words, if Tanya or I don't agree to fall in with this proposal of yours, then one of us is going to be fired, is that it?' she deduced, angrily caustic.

'Retrenched,' corrected Fraser in a hatefully goading drawl.

Rowan glared at him helplessly, wishing she could tell him to go ahead and be done with it, but while Tanya was watching with such a worried expression, she knew it was impossible to do so. Neither was her frustration helped in the slightest when she was only too aware just which one of them was going to have to accept the change of position. Not that she really wanted to remain in the factory because, if the truth were known, she would have preferred doing something that required a little more thought, but how could she expect Tanya to volunteer when it would mean that girl having to forgo the time Evan did manage to spend with her during the day?

'You don't believe in giving anyone much of a choice, do you?' she sniped bitterly, still unable to submit to the inevitable without some form of challenge.

'I thought I just had.' Fraser's gaze held hers provokingly.

Some choice! Rowan railed furiously. Either put herself under his almost constant surveillance, or else forfeit her employment altogether! And once having done the former, he probably intended to ensure that the latter swiftly followed anyway!

'So which one is it to be?'

The slightly impatiently worded but openly mocking question had Rowan's nails digging into the palms of her hands as they involuntarily clenched at her sides, but as if she guessed at the force of her friend's feelings on the matter, it was Tanya who began offering in a conciliatory fashion.

'I think maybe it had better be . . .'

'Me, I guess,' Rowan determinedly finished for her, and earned herself a partly grateful, partly anxious look from the other girl. With her head angled defiantly high, she made herself eye Fraser unwaveringly. 'So when am I supposed to start?'

'Now would seem as convenient a time as any,' he advised, pushing himself away from the counter.

Rowan shrugged and looked down at the pale pink uniform she was wearing. 'I'll have to change out of this.'

'I'll wait,' drily.

For longer than he was anticipating, though, she decided perversely as she headed for the change rooms. His grating victory wasn't going to be a complete walkover if she could help it.

'Rowan! Whatever's keeping you?' Tanya enquired doubtfully on entering the change rooms some considerable time later and seeing her friend leisurely combing her hair. 'You've got Fraser so riled he's threatening to come in here and haul you out himself!'

'So what's stopping him?' Rowan countered incorrigibly, continuing with what she was doing. 'It can't be his sensitivity, because he doesn't know the meaning of the word!'

Tanya didn't even attempt to debate that particular point. 'But you've been in here for almost half an hour!' she exclaimed instead.

'Well, he surely didn't expect me to change without showering first, did he?'

'A thirty-minute shower?' Tanya's lips curved ruefully. 'Besides, why shouldn't he? You know very well we don't usually shower before changing to go home. It's not as if the work we do is dirty, and with the factory being air-conditioned as well, there's never been any call for us to do so.'

'Until this afternoon,' Rowan grinned around the hairpins she was holding in her mouth while she tried to arrange her hair tidily on top of her head. However, since she wasn't used to dressing it in such a style her efforts weren't very successful and, letting the long strands fall about her shoulders, she replaced the pins in her bag and calmly began re-combing it.

'Rowan!' her companion immediately admonished agitatedly. 'You'll get us both the sack if you're not careful!'

'Hmm. . .?' came the considering response. Followed by a flippant, 'Okay, I guess I can't put off the fateful moment for ever, can I?' as she dropped her comb into her bag.

'You really dislike the idea of working up at the house to such an extent?'

'Well, I'm certainly not looking forward to it, I can tell you that much,' Rowan laughed expressively. 'Although I . . .' A thunderous pounding on the door brought her to a halt, her brows rising sardonically. 'I do believe we're being paged,' she quipped, and flinging open the door came face to face with Fraser's totally uncompromising features.

'At least that obtained some results!' he promptly rasped in wrathful tones.

'Results?' Rowan echoed artlessly. Then, with a wide-eyed look of supposed realisation, 'Oh, was all that banging a signal for us? I thought you were testing the door for evidence of termites.'

'Did you really!' he bit out with sarcastic savagery, grasping hold of her arm and already beginning to hustle her towards the outer doorway. 'Well, now perhaps you'd care to explain just what took you so long, you equivocating little liar!'

Rowan, of course, couldn't be quite so candid with her opinions, but since it appeared she had managed to get under his skin for once, she decided to continue in the same vein.

'Was I long?' she gazed innocently up at him to query. 'I'm so sorry if I kept you waiting, but naturally I couldn't consider changing without having a shower.'

A muscle jerked spasmodically at the side of Fraser's jaw, and thrusting aside the glass door he propelled her with markedly tightening fingers across to the jackaroo. 'No, naturally!' he grated. 'And especially not while I could be kept hanging around, hmm?'

'You didn't have to wait,' she asserted with a shrug. 'I could have made my own way up to the house.'

A well-shaped brow quirked cynically upwards. 'To arrive . . . when? Next week? Since it takes you more than thirty minutes just to change!'

'I've already apologised for that.'

'Yeah, so you have!' He swung open the door of the vehicle and all but pushed her inside before pacing around the front and climbing in beside her. Catching her off guard with the unexpectedness of the action, he abruptly captured her chin with an immobilising hand and lowered his head to within perturbing centimetres of hers. 'But if you so much as give me even one tiny reason to fault you again, honey, you can take my word for it that it'll be the last day you ever spend on this plantation!' His black-lashed eyes pinned her with an implacable grey gaze. 'Got the picture?'

'I got that a week ago!' she flared uncontrollably, all her provoking pretensions fast disappearing with his ultimatum. 'And this is the chance you've been waiting for ever since, isn't it? To put one of us in a position where you can continually find fault!'

'Uh-uh, not continually,' he vetoed, lazily mocking. 'It will only take another once.'

'Then why approve of Evan's employing us in the first place?'

He shrugged impassively. 'Because, at this stage, I figured acceptance would be more successful than resistance on my part in getting your friend out of his system.' With a taunting smile he set her free and switched on the ignition, then slanted her a superior, knowing glance. 'Nothing will ever come of their relationship, you know,' he advised ironically.

Rowan's brown eyes flashed with contempt. 'Because you plan to ensure it doesn't?' she gibed.

'Knowing my cousin as I do, I doubt if I'll have to,' he denied, aggravatingly confident.

'Meaning?' tautly. Just what was he getting at?

'That although Evan may appear very keen at the moment, he unfortunately—or perhaps in this instance I should say, fortunately,' he flicked her another of those goading glances, 'isn't exactly known for his—er—constancy when it comes to members of the opposite sex.'

Shades of Tanya! groaned Rowan in silent despair. It was demoralising to think that what she had suffered at Fraser's hands so far might yet prove to have all been for nothing, but simultaneously, she had no intention of disclosing any details regarding her friend's somewhat less than steadfast emotions to him either.

'Well, maybe this is the one time when he will be,' she proposed, as much to boost her own sinking feelings as to dampen his. 'Although, if what you contend is true,' as a suddenly alleviating suspicion occurred to her, 'there would have been no reason for you to keep trying to prevent them from seeing one another, would there?'

'Except a basic dislike of females who are obviously on the make!' he took his eyes briefly from the road ahead in order to impart in derogatory accents.

Rowan had never felt more like hitting someone in all her life, and it was only by forcefully reminding herself of the inevitable consequences of such an action that she managed to refrain. She was damned sure she wasn't going to be the one to provide Fraser with the cause for terminating their employment!

'Tanya is not on the make ... as you so enchantingly describe it,' she refuted between gritted teeth. 'She just happens to be attracted to Evan—as a person! Or is that so incomprehensible to you because material wealth happens to be *your* only yardstick?' She couldn't keep the corrosive note out of her voice altogether.

Fraser sent her an ominously hard-eyed and inflexible stare. 'Don't try shifting the direction of the conversation, honey,' he recommended tersely. 'It's not my motives that are under scrutiny here.'

'Because they're too noble ... or too questionable?'

she sniped before she could stop herself, and swallowed nervously on seeing the ominous levelling of his lips.

'Are you certain you wouldn't prefer to withdraw that remark?' he enquired coldly.

No, of course she didn't prefer to! But in the circumstances she didn't really have any option. 'I'm sorry,' she murmured with hardly disguised reluctance. 'But you shouldn't have said that about Tanya.'

'Why not? She's the one doing all the chasing, isn't she?'

'No!' She stared at him indignantly. 'It's been a—a mutual association.'

'Oh?' A crooking brow lent his features a cynical cast. 'Then I wonder why it required so little persuasion to have Evan passively agreeing to forgo her company on occasion? Hardly the behaviour you would expect of an infatuated lover, eh?' Both brows lifted in mocking unison now.

Were Tanya and Evan lovers? Rowan would have been surprised to discover that to be the case, aware as she was of her friend's attitude towards pre-marital sex, but rather than take Fraser to task on the point she accused hesitantly instead, 'I—I've only your word for it that he did accept your—your interference compliantly.' Since she herself had wondered much the same about Evan, it was difficult to evince an absolute conviction.

Evidently, Fraser deduced much the same from her tone too, for after bringing the vehicle to a halt beneath a shading jacaranda at the back of the house, he leant forward to rest sinewed brown forearms on the wheel and aimed an extremely shrewd gaze in her direction.

'But by the sound of it, that word was apparently

enough to convince you of the truth of it,' he guessed in heavily sardonic overtones.

'Hardly!' she managed to scoff, attempting to regain lost ground. 'After all, as well as being your cousin, Evan is also an employee of yours, and for all I know you could have threatened him with—er—retrenchment too, if he didn't accede to your wishes.'

'Highly unlikely, though, wouldn't you say?'

Rowan shook her head decisively. 'Where you're concerned, I'm afraid not. You forget, I already know from personal experience,' a trace of acrimony began creeping into her voice, 'the utterly unscrupulous methods you're willing to use in order to enforce your will on others.'

'And maybe I just suit the method to the person, because when you engage in suspect little ruses like you did, honey, you ask for whatever you get,' he contended peremptorily.

'Oh!' Her breasts rose and fell sharply beneath her cotton tank top. 'And your behaviour wasn't suspect, I suppose?'

Unexpectedly, Fraser suddenly grinned, impenitently, and to her annoyance had Rowan's pulse pounding traitorously in response. 'It's called fighting fire with fire,' he advised in a lazy drawl as he began opening his door.

Flinging wide her own door, Rowan was out of the vehicle in a flash and slamming the door resoundingly shut again almost before he had finished alighting. 'Well, that's a handy means of justifying your despicable actions, isn't it?' she threw at him across the hood. Followed by a sweetly gibing, 'I wonder if you'd find it as acceptable, though, if I used the same tactics against you.'

'You mean, if you started undressing me?' he

laughed, deliberately misunderstanding her. His eyes gleamed with lazy mockery. 'Be my guest.'

Rowan's cheeks flamed with embarrassment and she berated herself furiously for having resurrected the incident. 'That wasn't what I was meaning at all!' she flared. As if he didn't know! 'And—and, anyway,' her voice began to falter with selfconsciousness under his obviously amused glance and she averted her own gaze swiftly, 'I thought we were s-supposed to be discussing Tanya and—and Evan.'

'You were the one who saw fit to introduce other issues,' he reminded her drily.

A mistake she would never make again! she vowed determinedly. And seeking a less humiliating topic, tenaciously raised her eyes to his again to quiz sardonically, 'Well, are we going into the house, or do my duties start out here?'

'They won't start at all if you don't watch yourself,' came the prompt retort which had her chewing at her lip despondently and cursing her unruly tongue.

'I'm sorry,' she sighed, and wished, not for the first time, that Tanya could have chosen to fall for anyone other than Fraser Delaney's cousin. It would only be a matter of time before he found that one fault he was waiting for, but in the meantime . . . In the meantime, she repeated with strengthening resolve, squaring her shoulders, there was no way she was going to give him the satisfaction of knowing just how unbearable she found the situation to be.

Once inside the house, Fraser showed Rowan into a spacious, ultra-modern kitchen where his middle-aged housekeeper was seated at a rectangular table industriously slicing beans, her plastered leg resting on another chair.

'How's it going?' he asked immediately of the older woman.

'I guess I'll survive,' she smiled. 'But at least, and at last,' with a rueful chuckle, 'it's taught me not to walk on that marble floor while it's still wet.' Then, welcomingly, 'So it's you who's come to help me, is it, Rowan?'

'If you can put up with having me around,' Rowan half smiled diffidently. It was apparent others couldn't! 'And I was sorry to hear about your accident. Although shouldn't you really be resting completely?' accompanied by a somewhat accusing look in her employer's direction.

'Oh, no, that's what Fraser suggested, but I wouldn't hear of it,' Alice explained, unwittingly refuting Rowan's unspoken charge, and unaware of the taunting gaze Fraser promptly subjected the younger girl to. 'I'm not totally incapacitated and I'd much rather do *something*. I just need some assistance with those chores that require a fair amount of standing or walking, that's all.'

'Besides which , being such a perfectionist, she's loath to leave the house to somebody else's perhaps less than tender mercies,' put in Fraser wryly. 'She insists on keeping her finger on the pulse, as it were.'

'Do you blame me?' Alice countered, eyes twinkling. 'The last twice I've been on holidays, I don't think either of the temporary housekeepers we hired so much as touched a broom or a duster to the place during the whole time I was away, and it took me weeks to get it back to how it should be afterwards. And all because you and Evan are never in the house long enough to do any supervising!' She wagged a reproving finger at him.

With a warm attractive laugh, Fraser held up a hand in mock surrender. 'Uh—uh, we're not going into that again,' he drawled—rather enigmatically from Rowan's point of view. 'In any event,' his voice firmed to a surprising crispness, 'Rowan's friend is already doing her best to solve your problems in that regard. And now,' he inclined his head briefly, 'I'd better get back to work.'

However, it appeared he hadn't finished all he had to say yet, because at the doorway he stopped again in order to recommend arbitrarily, 'Oh, Rowan, I think it would be advisable for you to consider moving in here, at least for the next few weeks. I don't want Alice attempting to do too much due to your not having arrived, or because you've gone home.'

Rowan spluttered helplessly with shock, but by the time she had recovered sufficiently to give coherence to her mutinous thoughts, Fraser was already heading out through the back door and all she could do was to glare after his swiftly departing figure with impotent fury.

And just when had that idea occurred to him? she seethed. He hadn't seen fit to mention it earlier, of course! Well, the next time they met she'd be telling him exactly what she thought of his suggestion—no, order! she qualified hotly, for it had certainly been nothing less. If he thought for even one minute that she intended moving in under the same roof as himself, then he really had another think coming! Or was it herself who was due for another of those? she grimaced with sudden dejection.

When was she going to learn that while there was still Tanya to be considered, Fraser's word was tantamount to law where she was concerned? Granted, it might rankle, infuriate, and even affront, but as long as Tanya was so anxious for them to remain in the district, there wasn't a solitary thing Rowan could do about it. She could only save it all up and hope for a later date when it might be possible to vent her feelings to the full.

'Well, I certainly appeared to hit a sore point today, didn't I?' Alice's amused voice filtered through her reverie.

'I'm sorry? Oh, you mean, your remark about neither he nor Evan being in the house long enough to do any supervising?' Rowan speculated after dismissing her previous thoughts with a clearing shake of the head.

'Mmm, that's the one,' expressively.

Rowan eyed her curiously. 'As I recall, Fraser also said Tanya was doing her best to solve your problems in that regard,' she mused. 'What did he mean by that?'

'Not quite the same as I was implying, as he very well knows,' was the laughing, although no more enlightening, reply.

'I don't understand,' Rowan frowned.

'Oh, it's nothing very much,' Alice smiled, the knife in her hands continuing to slice rhythmically. 'I just keep telling him he ought to be married by now, or at least thinking about it, that's all. Considering all the work he puts into this place, it would be a shame if he didn't have children of his own to leave it to.'

Rowan couldn't quite agree. She was more inclined to think he was doing womankind a favour by not marrying! 'I'm still not sure what that has to do with supervising, though,' she said perplexedly.

'Well, if he had a wife there would be someone to keep an eye on the help when I'm away, wouldn't there?'

'Oh, I see,' Rowan nodded. 'And hence his comment concerning Tanya solving your problems for you.'

Alice's lips twitched wryly. 'Except it's not Evan I'm interested in seeing married.' Then, with a dismayed look, 'Oh, no offence meant to your friend, of course. She seems a very nice girl. But I guess there'll never be anyone quite like Fraser in my eyes.'

Rowan doubted there would be in hers either, only she suspected for very differing reasons! Although the other woman's remark did give her cause to probe with unaccountable interest, 'For any particular reason?'

'For reasons too numerous to mention.'

When it became evident that was to be the sum total of Alice's revelations, Rowan accepted her decision with good grace even though her newly whetted curiosity could hardly have been said to have been appeased. In fact, she was finding, somewhat to her alarm, that rather than disappearing, her interest seemed to be increasing owing to the lack of information, and, in an effort to eject Fraser from her thoughts entirely, she swiftly offered her services to Alice.

'Well, what would you like me to do to help?' she smiled with studied brightness.

Alice finished the last of the beans and laid the knife across the top of the bowl she had been slicing them into. 'You can put these in water, if you would, then these,' indicating a sheet of paper containing the scraps, 'can go in the garbage disposal as soon as I've done the peas.' She began emptying some plump green pods from a full plastic bag already on the table.

Relieving her of the beans, Rowan put the knife on the sink and began to absently fill the bowl with water. Until now, she had only read about kitchens like this. Garbage disposals, dishwashers, and microwave ovens—all articles she could see at a glance—were way out of Tanya's and her league, and although the hotel in Kurrawa Bay might have been similarly equipped, it was certainly the first time she had ever come across such an array of appliances in a private home. With a sigh of appreciation she turned off the water and, leaving the bowl on the sink, returned to the table to assist in shelling the peas.

'It's a beautiful house, isn't it?' she said, surmising the rest of it was probably no less impressive than the outside or the kitchen.

'Mmm, it certainly is,' Alice agreed wholeheartedly. 'And I'd show you around if it wasn't for that,' with an explicit glance at the cast on her leg, 'but if you'd like to have a wander through, to familiarise yourself with the place, so to speak, then go ahead. There's no one here except ourselves at the moment, so you're not likely to interrupt anyone.'

'But I'm supposed to be helping you,' Rowan felt bound to protest.

'Oh, I think I'll be able to manage without you for a while,' her objection was laughingly waved aside.

About to depart, Rowan promptly changed her mind and decided against it, her expression wry. 'No, I'd better not. It would be just my luck for Fraser to return during my absence.'

'So?' Alice's brows drew down over her kindly brown eyes.

'He—er—might think,' definitely would, most likely! 'I was trying to avoid doing any work.'

Those iron-grey brows flew skywards this time. 'Why on earth should he? You don't normally, do you?'

Rowan hunched one slender shoulder discomfitedly, unwilling to reveal too much. 'No—o ... but I wouldn't like to give him any cause for complaint either.'

'Because, since you volunteered to help out in the house, you would obviously prefer to work here rather than in the factory?'

Rowan jumped gratefully at the excuse offered, although hearing the reasoning behind it did have her lips curving sardonically. So she was supposed to have volunteered for the position, was she? It had felt more as if she'd been commandeered for it, to her!

'Yes, well, I really would rather do something that required a little more thought,' she owned hastily. Which was perfectly true, even if she did wish the job had been anywhere else but in Fraser's own house. 'So you see, if he did think I wasn't helping as much as I should, he'd probably send me back to the factory.' Which wasn't quite as truthful, since she had no doubt that under those circumstances he'd have no compunction in summarily terminating her employment altogether.

'Then if that's all that's bothering you, you have absolutely nothing to worry about, believe me!' Alice impressed on her earnestly. 'Or don't you think I'd tell Fraser—*if* he returned, which I might add, is most improbable at this time of the day—that it was at my suggestion you were looking over the house?'

'Oh, naturally I assumed you would,' Rowan confirmed hurriedly. Alice had begun to sound a little piqued at the last. 'But—er—more to the point ... would he approve of the explanation?'

'Well, of course he would!' The older woman sounded definitely rattled now. 'I don't know whatever's the matter with you that you should be so nervous of Fraser's reaction. You're making him out to be a positive ogre, although I can't possibly fathom why! I've worked here for almost sixteen years now, so I know for a fact that you couldn't find a less ogre-like employer than Fraser—or his father before him—if you tried.'

Hell! Rowan despaired. Now she'd succeeded in riling Alice too. It was apparent that if she was to remain in the housekeeper's good graces, then she would be better served by keeping her comments regarding Fraser to the barest, least critical, minimum.

'I'm sorry,' she smiled remorsefully. 'That really wasn't what I intended to imply.' She hadn't meant to imply *anything*, actually! 'I was just wary that my actions might have been misconstrued, that's all.'

'But not, as I said, while I'm here to defend them.' It was a categorical statement.

'I—I was forgetting that. I'm sorry,' Rowan apologised yet again. It seemed to be an expression for which she had had an increasing use today!

'Yes, well, let's say no more about it, shall we?' Alice smiled, regaining her usual good humour. 'You just go ahead and let me worry about any explanations, if necessary, eh?'

'All right . . . and thank you,' Rowan welcomed the offer of a truce with a reciprocal smile. 'I won't be long.'

Alice waved her away with one hand. 'After what you've just been saying, you think I don't know that already?' she countered in dry accents.

With a grin, Rowan made for the doorway that led into the hall.

Twenty minutes later, after having wandered leisurely through every imposing and superbly furnished room on the ground floor—there was even a watered silk-lined ballroom, for heaven's sake!—she stood for a moment on the beautifully veined marble floor of the foyer—where Alice had fallen only that morning, presumably—glancing wonderingly at the elegance that surrounded her, and fingering almost reverently the giant newel-post of the magnificent cedar staircase that rose in carved splendour to the galleries above.

Certainly she had never before been in a house that even nearly approached the size of this one, and it was impossible for her to imagine what it would feel like to either own such a place, or to call something so grand home. The last word had her thoughts turning inward involuntarily. That was the worst part, she'd always found, of having no family of her own. There was never the security of knowing you had somewhere to return to—of having somewhere to call home.

CHAPTER FOUR

'WELL, how did it go?' asked Tanya watchfully later that evening. Rowan had only just made it back to Mrs Raymond's in time for dinner, and throughout the meal the darker-haired girl had sensed that her friend wasn't in a particularly contented frame of mind. However, now that they had reached the privacy of Rowan's room, the prudent curbing of her impatience which she had shown during dinner could be dispensed with.

Rowan stopped sorting through her wardrobe long enough to give a shrug and wry grimace in response. 'Do you mean before, or after, I almost got myself fired?' she quipped.

'Oh, you didn't!' Tanya exclaimed, aghast. 'How?'

'Because I suggested his motives for employing us were too questionable to bear scrutiny.'

'But what in heaven's name made you say such a thing? You know Evan explained all that the day he brought us here.'

She also knew what Fraser had had to say on the matter too, but since his remarks hadn't been very complimentary to her companion, Rowan didn't really feel like repeating them.

'Yes, well, I guess Evan's cousin just has the unhappy knack of rubbing me up the wrong way all the time,' she parried as she withdrew a full-length printed skirt and a waistcoat-styled blouse from the wardrobe.

Diverted for the moment, Tanya watched her

curiously. 'What are you getting those out for?'

'So I can wear them,' drily.

'Tomorrow?'

'Tonight.'

'O—h?' Tanya drew the word out meaningfully, eyes gleaming. 'And just who are you going out with, might I ask?'

'You may,' allowed Rowan humorously, laying her clothes on the other end of the bed to where her friend was sitting, and then collecting some toiletries preparatory to heading for the bathroom. 'But as it so happens, I'm not going *with* anyone. I just thought that as you and Evan are going to the movies in Southleigh,' the largest town in the area situated farther inland, 'I would take myself off to the Bay for the evening. As you know, the Crossroads isn't exactly famed for its hectic night life, and after the events of today, believe me, I feel like letting off some steam.'

'Then why not come to the movies with us?'

Rowan shook her head wryly. 'Thank you for the offer . . . but no, thanks. I've never played gooseberry before and I don't intend to start now.'

Tanya sighed resignedly, knowing from her tone that her friend's mind was made up. 'But how will you get there? I thought there was only one bus every morning from Southleigh to the Bay that comes through here.'

'Mmm, so I understand,' Rowan murmured vaguely, unconcernedly, as she searched for the gold chain necklace she wanted to wear. It was the only really decent piece of jewellery she owned. 'In any case, I was thinking of thumbing a ride. There always seems to be plenty of cars heading in that direction.'

Tanya nodded thoughtfully. Although hitch-hiking wasn't a method of transport they favoured, it was one they'd used on a number of occasions—happily, without incident—when their finances had been almost non-existent. 'And you expect to be able to get a lift back again just as easily?' she quizzed.

'I'll think about that when the time arrives,' Rowan suddenly grinned.

'But what will you do if you can't get a ride home?'

'Think about that if and when it's necessary too, I suppose.'

'Rowan! I'm serious!' Tanya burst out chidingly.

'So am I,' was the partly apologetic, partly defiant return. 'Because right at the moment I've had Fraser Delaney and his insufferable dictates up to here!' touching the back of one hand to her chin. 'But of course, you haven't heard his latest one yet, have you?' Rowan smouldered, beginning to pace angrily about the room. And without waiting for an answer, she went on, 'Well, it seems our dearly beloved boss has arbitrarily decided that I'd be of more help to Alice if I not only work in the house, but move in there as well!'

Momentarily, Tanya sat in stunned silence, then queried in a somewhat tentative voice, 'And is that when—when you accused him of having—er—questionable motives?'

'No, we'd already been through that!' she was informed tersely. 'This one was given out in front of Alice. Probably in order to make me look callous and selfish when I objected, which he knew I would, except I wasn't given a chance to.'

'I'm not sure I follow you,' Tanya frowned. 'Did you or didn't you object?'

Rowan combed her fingers irritably through her hair. 'No, I didn't object,' she sighed. 'He walked out before I had an opportunity to open my mouth.

Anyway, what would have been the use?' she added moodily. 'He knows as well as I do that even if I had objected, I don't really have any option but to agree in the end because he's the one holding all the aces.'

'Then perhaps I should have taken the job, after all. I wouldn't have minded so much having to live in the same house as Evan,' Tanya tried lifting her companion's spirits with a faint show of humour.

'Maybe not,' Rowan conceded ironically. Although she privately doubted even someone as easygoing as Tanya could suffer Fraser's brand of highhandedness for very long. Not and remain unscathed, that was! She added a towel to her other requisites and raised one shoulder in a dismissive shrug. 'But that's another story, and meanwhile, time is slipping by. So I'll see you in the morning, I expect,' she finished, reaching for the door handle.

'I certainly hope so!' laughed Tanya expressively as she accompanied her into the hall. Her expression sobered a little. 'But when will you be moving, Rowan? Tomorrow?'

'Not if I have anything to do with it! I'll be taking as long as I possibly can before obeying that presumptuous decree, believe me!'

Rowan stopped for a while on the outskirts of town, debating whether she should wait where she was or keep walking. Of course, any drivers who happened along would be able to see her from a greater distance if she stayed within the circle of light thrown by the last street lamp, but tonight she felt too restless and edgy to remain patiently in the one place, so she decided to continue walking. Or perhaps stumbling would have been a more accurate description, she concluded ruefully after only a hundred metres or so, for in the darkness which now surrounded her it was difficult to see just exactly where the road was, and every time she tripped on the broken edges and found herself lurching along the stony sides instead, she blessed the foresight that had made her wear low-heeled sandals.

Even so, by the time she was only half way round the sweeping curve she remembered from when they'd arrived in town, she was starting to wonder if it wouldn't have been wiser to have stayed under the lamp after all. A car speeding past and going in her direction, but without so much as slowing at her signal, made the choice for her. She stopped and turned, but before she could begin retracing her steps she was caught in the glare of another set of approaching headlights. However, on this occasion the car came to a rubber-burning stop just in front of her and she hurried up to it gratefully.

'Thanks very much,' she began as she opened the passenger door. 'I was . . .'

'What the bloody hell do you think you're doing?' A savage voice stopped her in her tracks, and looking into the interior Rowan discovered herself to be staring straight into Fraser's icily glittering grey eyes.

'Seeing you stopped, I would have thought that was obvious,' she shrugged.

'Are you mad? Don't you know the sort of trouble you're letting yourself in for by thumbing a ride on a lonely road like this at night? Where in blazes are you going, anyway?'

Stung by his unwanted censure, she lifted her chin defiantly. 'To the Bay.'

'At this time of night? What on earth for?'

Not that it was any of his business, but . . . 'Because I felt like it,' she retorted acidly.

His shapely mouth levelled tautly. 'Why didn't you get someone to drive you down, then?'

'That's what I was attempting to do when you stopped,' she smiled with facetious sweetness.

'I meant somebody you know!' he grated.

'Because I don't like going around asking people if . . .'

'No, you'd rather put yourself at risk by asking a stranger!' he cut in on her irately again. 'Of all the stupid . . .!' He stifled an expletive and then cast her a heavily exasperated glance. 'Well, are you going to get in, or are you going to stand there all night?'

Rowan decided the latter was the preferable of the two. 'I'm sorry to have bothered you, but I think I'll wait for someone else to come along, thanks all the same,' she replied on a somewhat sarcastic note, and closing the door, began heading back the way she'd come.

'*Rowan*! Get yourself back here!'

Ignoring the infuriated summons, she continued on her way—but only until she heard the unexpected sound of swift footsteps behind her, whereupon she spun around with a challenging look already settling on her delicate features.

'You senseless, perverse, damned idiot!' Fraser castigated scathingly as he grabbed hold of her arm before she could evade him and gave her a furious shake. 'Either you get in that car, or I'll throw you in it!'

'No!' she flouted stormily, resentfully, and struggling ineffectually against the hand that was hauling her inexorably towards the vehicle. 'You can't tell me what to do out of working hours!'

'Don't you believe it!' The recommendation was roughly made as he pulled the car door open.

'No, you can't!' she continued to defy even as she was being forced towards the seat. 'I don't have to accept a lift from you if I don't want to. And I *don't* want to! I'd much rather ... Oh!' she finished indignantly, when both her vocal and physical objections were totally disregarded and she was bundled into the vehicle anyway.

'And make sure you damned well stay there, or we're likely to have some fool come haring round that corner and wipe us all out before very much longer!' Fraser slammed the door shut behind her and stalked around to the driver's side.

His disconcerting prediction was the only thing that kept Rowan seated, but when he slid his muscular length on to the seat next to her and quickly set the car in motion again, she sent him one baleful glare and then concentrated her gaze on the black ribbon of road easily visible now in the bright illumination provided by the headlights. Superior strength might have enabled him to force her into the car, but it couldn't make her acknowledge his presence.

'So how far were you planning to walk if you hadn't got a ride? All the way?' he queried in a satirical drawl.

Oh, yes, now that he'd managed to compel her into submitting to his wishes once again, he could afford to make fun of her! Rowan railed inwardly. Outwardly, she gave a haughty sniff and maintained a stony silence.

'Well?' with a little more bite in his tone.

She turned her head slowly, her eyes dark and rebellious but extremely eloquent as they connected briefly with his, and then just as deliberately she resumed her previous position without having uttered a word.

'Oh, stop being so childish!' he immediately slated. 'You wanted a lift, and you got one. You're lucky it was me who happened along and not somebody with less favourable ideas in mind.'

'*Lucky!*' The scornful gibe burst forth spontaneously despite her resolve to remain silent. 'Forcing an unwilling person into a car and then driving off with them constitutes kidnap, you know!'

'When you're being driven where you want to go?' He raised a mocking brow.

'That still doesn't give you the right to ignore what I want!'

'But I thought that was . . . to go to the Bay.'

'With someone of *my* choosing!'

He slanted her a sardonic gaze at that. 'I'd hardly call it your choice when you're willing to hop in the first vehicle you manage to flag down.'

Rowan moved restively beneath his disturbing grey gaze. 'Tanya and I have refused lifts we've been offered before now,' she relayed, defensively defiant.

'But only you would be so contrary as to refuse one from somebody you know, just because you were criticised for hitch-hiking at all!'

'It wasn't just because of that.' She annoyingly found herself having to justify her actions once more. 'Even though it's nothing to do with you how I choose to obtain transport,' she couldn't resist inserting. 'But I knew you'd only stopped because you'd really wanted to, and—and I don't intend having you ordering me around during my time off as well as at work!'

'No?' Strangely, her remarks had put a steely ring back in his voice again. 'Well, if I ever hear of you trying to thumb a ride again, I'll do more than just order you around!' he threatened. 'There'll be hell to pay, believe me!'

Feelings of outrage rampaged through Rowan

uncontrollably. 'You've no right to . . .!'

'I've just assumed the right, since you're obviously either too naïve or too pigheaded to see the dangers involved!' Fraser cut her off harshly.

'I'll—I'll . . .!' she choked helplessly.

'You'll either go with someone, or else ask for the use of one of the plantation vehicles in future!' he retorted.

Under other circumstances, she supposed she might have been grateful for the concession, but as it was . . . 'And much good that'll do me! I don't happen to be able to drive!' she hurled back at him.

Fraser muttered something unprintable beneath his breath. 'Then if you plan on going anywhere while you're working at the plantation, I might suggest you learn . . . fast!'

'What would be the point?' she shrugged with a sudden, and unaccustomed, spiritlessness. 'You've made it plain, right from the outset, that we weren't welcome, and I know you'll get rid of us the minute you think you can do so without displeasing Evan.'

'Although not while Alice is incapacitated, of course.'

'Oh, no, now that one of us is of some use to you it's a different matter, isn't it?' the mocking drawl had her snapping back bitterly.

In the darkness his teeth gleamed whitely in a lazily evocative smile she found infinitely disturbing. But whether that was due to her errant senses waywardly reacting to his intense masculinity, or just selfconsciousness on her part, she didn't care to examine too closely.

'You, honey, I could always find some use for, I'm sure,' he imparted with a significantly encompassing glance.

Rowan flushed hotly, although mainly with embarrassment rather than anger, she realised abruptly to her consternation, but certain any remonstrance from her would only bring about another humiliating reference concerning her grievous visit to the beach house, she determinedly refused to utter any retaliation which could present him with such an opportunity.

Instead, and as a result of her own recollection, she was prompted to query protectively, as well as a trifle suspiciously, 'A-anyway, how come you've been back at the plantation this week? I thought you were still supposed to be on holiday.'

As if well aware of the reasoning behind her sudden change of subject, Fraser grinned tauntingly. 'Sorry to disappoint you, but I decided to cut them short.'

'Immediately you discovered Evan had offered us employment, no doubt!' she grimaced.

'I couldn't bear the thought of you being out of my sight.'

Couldn't bear the thought of missing a chance to find fault, he meant! she interpreted caustically, and retreated into a defensive silence once more.

Soon the road began its gradual descent to the coastal plains and it was possible to see the lights of the Bay below them—a sight which had Rowan sighing with relief. Quite apart from his strictures, in the close confines of the car she was finding Fraser's company too disruptive to her peace of mind and she wouldn't be at all sorry when their journey came to an end.

In more ways than one, he was certainly the most unsettling male she had ever encountered, although she was none too certain just why that should have been the case. Admittedly, he was also one of the most physically attractive she had ever met, but since mere

good looks had never caused her heart rate to increase
before, she was at something of a loss to explain why
his should apparently have the power to demolish her
composure so effortlessly now.

'So when do you expect to be moving up to the
house?' Fraser's somewhat dry-sounding query
suddenly interrupted the quiet.

Recalling that that very suggestion had been the
main motive for her deciding to hitch-hike to the Bay,
Rowan snapped out of her introspective mood quickly,
and with her temper on the rise. 'Now that you come
to mention it, I have absolutely no idea, actually,' she
just managed to smile, provokingly, between gritted
teeth. 'You did only say I should *consider* moving up
there, didn't you?'

'Mmm,' he conceded laconically. 'Consider . . . and
then comply.'

In other words, it had been an order! Just as she'd
known it had been. 'Oh, how dense of me, I didn't
realise. I thought you were giving me a choice,' she
warbled in an assumed artlessness which took some
considerable effort. She was as mad as a hornet
underneath! 'Now I guess I shall have to give it some
thought, after all, won't I?'

'Don't bother,' she was counselled in sardonic
tones. 'Just do it . . . tomorrow.'

Momentarily, Rowan forgot the role she was playing
and flared, 'No, I . . .'

'Tomorrow!' Fraser promptly repeated insistently.

Rowan could have screamed with frustration. 'Do
you always have to be quite so damned unyielding?'
she complained defeatedly, then caught her lip
between even white teeth in dismay because she really
hadn't intended to voice her despair out loud.

Fraser grinned indolently. As she supposed *he*

could! 'That depends, I guess, on just how tolerant you expect me to be.'

'Well, that settles that!' she muttered, pulling a disgruntled face. She didn't anticipate any indulgence whatsoever. Then, in surprise, as he took a left turn instead of continuing on to the centre of town, 'Hey! Where are we going? If you're heading for your beach house, you can let me out here. It's not so far to walk.'

'Don't panic!' His lips slanted wryly. 'I have to collect someone and I'm late already.'

Curiosity overcame her desire to deny being alarmed. 'Someone ... female?' she just had to enquire, but couldn't understand the sharp stab of discontent she experienced when he nodded his affirmation. She hurried on swiftly, 'You don't think she'll find it a little odd, you arriving with me in tow?'

'I shouldn't think so. Erica's adult enough not to jump to the wrong conclusions.'

Whereas *her* reactions were childish in his opinion, Rowan recalled vexedly. 'Is that her name ... Erica?' She decided she didn't think she liked the sound of it.

'Mmm, Erica Melville,' he enlightened. 'She designs beachwear for her own boutique here in the Bay.'

'Oh, Melville's. I know it,' Rowan partly nodded, partly grimaced. As she remembered, every article in the shop had been far too pricey for either her or Tanya to even contemplate buying anything there. She slanted him a sideways look from the cover of long, dark lashes, an imp of mischief making her ask, 'And is she also adult enough to accept that you're ...' now how had he put it when referring to Evan? 'not exactly known for your—er—constancy when it comes to members of the opposite sex?'

Whether he recognised the wording or not, Rowan

didn't know, but she suddenly found herself on the receiving end of an extremely penetrating grey gaze. 'Meaning?' he prompted, briefly watchful.

'Oh, only that since you obviously like a variety when it comes to female companions, I couldn't help wondering if she objected to being just one in a long, long line,' she relayed airily. 'I mean, even while Tanya and I were at the Bay, you were rarely seen with the same girl twice.'

'But when I was, I was no doubt with Erica,' she was informed in rather mocking accents. 'Although, just what business is that of yours?'

'None at all,' she owned, shrugging aside another of those unaccountable twinges of dissatisfaction. By now they were winding their way along the headland which curved around the northern end of the beach, and which Rowan knew was dotted with the newest and most expensive homes in Kurrawa Bay. 'Is this where she lives?' she asked as Fraser brought the car to a halt near some steps leading down to a large Spanish style house below them.

'Uh-huh.' He opened his door and set one foot to the road.

Rowan did the same on her side. 'Well, thanks for the lift. I'll take the path down the cliff back there,' gesturing over her shoulder, 'and walk along the beach to town.'

'You can stay exactly where you are!' promptly came the vetoing command. 'I won't be long.' A pause, wherein his gaze sought hers across the roof of the car and his firmly shaped lips tilted ruefully, and then, 'Come to that, maybe I should keep an eye on you all evening. At least that way I'll know what you're up to,' as if it was any of his business, anyway! she fumed, 'and no doubt you'll need transport home again afterwards.'

While in the meantime, she was supposed to make up a cosy threesome together with himself and the unknown Erica, was she? Well, no way! she vowed vehemently. She'd already refused a similar offer from Tanya, but somehow she found the idea of being the odd one out with Fraser and his girl-friend even less palatable. Not that she intended revealing as much right at the moment, however. She wasn't going to risk having her wishes overruled yet again that evening.

'Okay,' she agreed with pretended acquiescence. 'I'll just get in the back, though, so your—er—companion can sit in the front.' She closed one door and started to open the other.

Fraser viewed her unexpectedly submissive movements with suspiciously narrowed eyes, but on seeing her slip on to the rear seat, he merely sent her one last measuring glance and repeated, 'We won't be long,' before turning and heading down the stone steps.

Rowan immediately slid out of the vehicle again and closed the door, but cautiously waited until Fraser had disappeared from sight behind some gaudily flowering hibiscus bushes. Then, with a distinctly pleased look on her face, she headed for the path leading down the cliff face.

In the dark her descent proved to be a rather more precarious undertaking than it was in the bright light of day, and one which required all her concentration to ensure she didn't miss her footing, so it wasn't until she had managed to reach the sand below without mishap and turned her steps in the direction of the Esplanade that her mind could occupy itself with those thoughts it was apparently most eager to deliberate.

How dared Fraser even begin to think he had any

right to tell her what to do during her time off! All right, so maybe she had been a little foolish in saying she would have preferred to wait for somebody else when he'd first stopped, but considering his dictatorial attitude had been the reason for her wanting a change of scene for the evening, surely that wasn't so surprising! But then to have the unmitigated hide to suggest he should keep her under surveillance—in order to see what she was up to, for heaven's sake!— well, that was just the last straw!

And for your information, Fraser Delaney, she mouthed inaudibly but fervently into the warm, fragrant night air, you won't be providing me with any transport home again either, because if I don't find someone else going that way I'd rather sleep on the beach and catch the early morning bus travelling through to Southleigh than suffer two chafing trips with you in the one day!

'Hey, Rowan! Where did you spring from? I thought you and Tanya left town on your way north a week ago,' exclaimed a tall, dark-haired girl on noticing Rowan approaching the mixed group of young people she was with on the Esplanade.

'No, we've been working at the nut factory,' she explained with a smile, waving a hand in the general direction of the plantation.

'Sounds appropriate for you two,' quipped a male voice, and had them all laughing.

'Where is Tanya, anyway? Isn't she with you?' asked the same girl once the merriment had subsided a little.

Rowan shook her head. 'No, Evan's taken her to the movies in Southleigh tonight, Aileen.'

'She's still dating him, then?' put in Dawn, another of the girls.

'Mmm, why else do you think we're working at the Delaney factory?' with a rueful laugh.

'If it was me, in the hope that gorgeous hunk of a cousin of his might notice me.' Dawn rolled her blue eyes expressively.

Mention of Fraser had Rowan hunching both honey-toned shoulders in a dispassionate movement. 'And if he did, it would probably only be to order you around. Fraser's great with orders,' she relayed sardonically.

'As long as he paid me some attention, he could give me all the orders he liked,' maintained Dawn on an exaggerated sigh of imagined bliss at the thought.

Meanwhile, Aileen had been eyeing Rowan speculatively. 'Did I detect a note of vexation in that remark, by any chance?' she now quizzed quietly from the corner of her mouth.

Reluctant to go into details, Rowan schooled her features into an unconcerned smile. 'No, not really,' she whispered back, slightly less than truthfully. 'He just gives a few too many for my liking, nothing more. Really, I suppose I should be grateful for having any work at all instead of complaining. For a while there it didn't look as if we would have until Evan suggested the factory.' And seizing the opportunity to direct the conversation away from herself, indicated the whole group of a dozen or so, and rushed on to enquire, 'How about the rest of you?' Although the majority of them were locals, including Aileen, and were permanently employed by various businesses in the town, the rest were only temporary staff the same as Tanya and herself had been.

Aileen shrugged negligently. 'Oh, most of us are still doing much the same, although Geraldine's still at the hotel, I believe. I think there's some talk of them keeping her on as a relief receptionist. Bernie and Damien,' she gestured towards two of the young men at the back of the group as they all continued ambling along the street, 'have been put off, though. They're just sort of hanging around at the moment in the hope something else will turn up.'

'And Jerry?' Rowan named the last of their particular number she'd worked alongside at the hotel.

'You'll never guess!' Aileen almost choked with sudden laughter. 'He's got himself a job on one of the local fishing trawlers!'

'But he gets seasick if you just *talk* about water!' Rowan half gurgled, half gasped, and turned automatically to look at the bespectacled youth in question, who was walking a few paces behind them.

He immediately guessed the cause of their mirth and included them both in a mock threatening look. 'You just watch it, you pair!' he warned. 'At least it's gainful employment.'

'Oh? They need someone to hang over the side all the time, do they?' Aileen bantered, and went into another fit of laughter at her own joke.

Jerry's lips twisted grudgingly in response. 'Well, it's worth a try,' he grinned. 'If I can get used to it, I reckon it'd be a good life.'

'What on earth made you want to try it, though, knowing what it does to you?' inserted Rowan in a more serious manner.

'Oh, I don't know,' he shrugged and smiled wryly. 'I never said *I* didn't like the sea, just that the *sea* doesn't seem to like me.'

'And if you don't get used to it?'

His smile widened ruefully. 'Then I suspect the boss will politely suggest I seek work elsewhere.'

'Oh!' she acknowledged on an eloquent note, but had no time to add anything further as her attention was distracted by Aileen.

'Well, here we are!' the other girl exclaimed, coming to a halt outside the older, but less impersonal, Kurrawa Bay Hotel. She looked at Rowan questioningly. 'You're coming in with us, aren't you?'

'That was the general idea,' Rowan nodded. 'Is there anything in particular on?'

'A cabaret in the Fern Room,' one of the other men, Trevor, told her as he overheard. Draping one arm about her shoulders and another around Aileen, he began ushering them both inside. 'From what I hear, it's supposed to be very good.'

The Fern Room was the larger of the two entertainment areas the hotel possessed and, not surprisingly, in view of its name, was attractively decorated with a multitude of urns and hanging baskets filled with every type of fern imaginable. It also had the advantage of one whole wall being constructed entirely of sliding glass doors which when opened to the sea breezes, as they were now, prevented the area from ever becoming too hot or stuffy, and it was to this side of the room that Trevor led everyone after skirting those tables which were already occupied, three of the vacant tables then being pushed together in order to make one large one so they could all take a seat.

From her place between Trevor and Aileen, Rowan let her gaze drift casually round the room, noting the rapidly filling tables and the number of couples dancing to the music provided by the hotel's resident band from the stage situated at one end of the room.

'Well, this certainly seems to be the most popular place in town tonight,' she remarked to them

generally. 'Isn't there anything on at the Shore?' A
hint of a frown crossed her forehead as she mentioned
the other hotel. If everyone was patronising the
Kurrawa Bay this evening, then wasn't there a distinct
possibility that Fraser and his girl-friend might too?
And especially since the owner was apparently a good
friend of his!

'Nothing we haven't already seen,' Trevor answered
her query with a shrug.

Rowan breathed a little easier. The entertainment at
the Shore was usually of a good standard, so perhaps
they were going there. That was, of course, if they
didn't prefer to spend the evening on their own. She
dismissed the unwelcome thought angrily. Why
should she care how or where Fraser occupied his time
with Erica as long as he was nowhere within sight of
herself?

'What'll you have to drink, Rowan? Vodka . . . gin?'
Trevor's enquiry had her shaking her head
vigorously. The memory of the last occasion on which
she'd drunk the latter was still too vivid for comfort.
'Neither! I'll have one of the hotel's Specials, thanks,'
she declared decisively. She'd had them before and
although she might not have known just what
ingredients they contained, more importantly, she did
know they were long and refreshing, and not overly
intoxicating.

Presently, with their orders filled by a passing
waiter, the conversation continued along desultory
lines as they waited for the show to start, until Rowan
suddenly felt Aileen nudging her surreptitiously.

'Look!' She nodded imperceptibly towards the
stage. 'Isn't that your boss at that table with Sean
Goddard and company?'

Rowan's brown eyes darted swiftly in the same

direction, then closed for a moment in dismay. 'So it is,' she confirmed with a rueful moue, and shrinking further behind Trevor in the hope of avoiding any return detection.

Aileen didn't appear to notice the action. 'And that's Erica Melville with him, isn't it?'

The striking-looking redhead in the glamorous cream silk outfit who was almost sitting in his lap! Rowan presumed with unusual acrimony. 'I wouldn't know,' she denied protectively. 'I've never seen her before.' Well, she hadn't!

'Mmm, that's who it is all right,' Aileen nodded musingly. Then, to Rowan's dismay, she looked at the girl opposite to quiz, 'Isn't it, Dawn?'

The younger, fair-haired girl broke off her conversation with Jerry to glance back at her with enquiringly raised brows. 'Isn't what ... what?' she half laughed, half frowned.

'Isn't that Erica Melville down there with Fraser Delaney?' repeated Aileen.

'What! You mean, my favourite spunk's here tonight?' Dawn exclaimed ecstatically, just as Rowan had expected, and swinging around to make certain for herself. 'Why didn't someone tell me before? Oh, isn't he just divine? I've had a crush on him since I was ten years old, you know.'

'We wouldn't have guessed,' laughed Geraldine wryly from beside her. It was common knowledge among all of them that there was only one man in young Dawn's life—even if he had, so far, proved unattainable. 'Besides, you're not old enough for him, anyway.'

'I'm almost nineteen!'

'In another eight months,' interposed Aileen knowledgeably.

'Good lord, the girl's positively ancient,' teased Jerry drily from the ripe old age of twenty-two. 'Although I do wish she wouldn't breathe quite so heavy when she's talking about the feller. She keeps fogging up my glasses.' And removing them, he pretended to give them a wipe.

Dawn accepted their bantering comments in good part, but it was left to Aileen to finally remind her, 'You still haven't said whether that's Erica Melville with him or not yet.'

'Oh, yes, that's the stuck-up Miss Melville,' was the sardonically voiced affirmation, followed by an irrepressibly giggled, 'I mean, haven't you noticed the way she gives you the once-over whenever you walk into that shop of hers? If you haven't got a fat cheque book in your hand, she looks at you as if she'd like to sweep you out along with the rest of the dirt.'

'Your Fraser doesn't appear to have any complaints regarding her attitude,' put in Trevor slyly, and laughed when she pulled a face at him in retaliation.

'He isn't *my* Fraser,' Dawn denied, noticeably mournful. 'I only wish he was.' She looked hopefully across the table. 'You couldn't arrange an introduction for me, I suppose, Rowan? You're the only person I know who actually knows him.'

From trying to steer well clear of the conversation— she didn't even want to think about Fraser, let alone talk about him!—Rowan now found herself catapulted back into it again with a vengeance, and she stared at the other girl, aghast.

'Uh-uh! Sorry,' she recovered quickly to refuse with a wry half smile, but no less definitely for all that. 'He's my boss, not a friend.' Most assuredly he wasn't the latter! she added mutely. 'In any event, I hardly think it would be appropriate while there's another female already clinging to him like a leech.' A few uncontrollable but covert glances had shown Erica to have her arm linked almost constantly with his.

Dawn sighed and wrinkled her nose disappointedly. 'I guess you're right. Although maybe . . .'

The entrance of the show's compère on to the stage had her stopping in mid-sentence—much to Rowan's relief, because she'd been dreading just what might have been suggested next—and the matter was fortunately forgotten during the cabaret performance.

It was late when the show finally finished and Rowan immediately began preparing to leave. She was determined she wasn't going back with Fraser, even if his offer did still hold good after she'd run out on him like she had, but she thought that if she was to get a ride with somebody else then she would be wise to find one as soon as possible.

'But you can't go now! The dancing's about to start,' protested Aileen on hearing her intention to leave. 'At least stay for a little while.'

'I would if I could,' Rowan smiled ruefully. 'Unfortunately, though, when you're hitch-hiking you have to be on the road when most of the traffic is, and as I figure about now will be my best chance of getting a lift, I'm afraid I don't really have much choice.' She carefully omitted to mention that she'd already been offered one.

From the other end of the table Damien suddenly entered the conversation. 'Are you after a lift to Southleigh, Rowan?' he asked in slightly befuddled accents. He and Bernie had been steadily drinking throughout the show.

'Not quite that far, just to the Crossroads,' she qualified.

'Well, if you'd like to stay in town tonight, Bernie

and I can take you in the morning. We're going to Southleigh first thing.'

It was certainly tempting, for although she would never have admitted as much to Fraser, she really didn't like having to thumb lifts. However, there was one problem . . .

'You can stay at my house if you want,' offered Aileen, their thoughts seemingly attuned. 'Mum won't mind. She's used to me having friends stay overnight.'

It was starting to sound better all the time, although Rowan still queried, 'You're sure?' And after receiving a series of emphatic nods in confirmation, to Damien, 'How early's first thing?'

'Hmm . . .' He fixed Bernie with a squinting gaze, but when that man only shrugged unconcernedly, specified, 'Sixish. That suit you?'

'Oh, yes,' her concurrence was readily given. That would certainly get her back to the plantation in plenty of time. 'Provided, of course, you'll both be awake by then,' she couldn't resist adding as she eyed the number of empty glasses in front of them with a humorously significant gaze.

'Don't you worry about us,' he retorted drily. 'We'll be there.' He gave a short laugh. 'Feeling a bit sorry for ourselves, maybe, but we will be there.'

'Okay, and thank you,' she laughed back.

'And now, since you're staying, how about a dance?' Trevor looked at her enquiringly. The band had resumed playing some time before.

'You've got yourself a partner,' she accepted gaily, and accompanied him on to the already filling dance floor.

And so it continued for the next hour and more. Rowan had always been a popular member of their group, and although she was sublimely unaware of the fact, there wasn't a man among them who wouldn't have considered it a feather in his cap if she'd displayed a preference for any one of them, but to their individual disappointment she treated them all exactly the same—as good friends only.

For Rowan's part, she had no interest in becoming romantically involved with anyone at the moment, and it had certainly never occurred to her that she only needed to walk into a room to have every male glance drawing instinctively in her direction, so it was with no little astonishment during one of the rare times she wasn't dancing to see Sean Goddard, the hotel's extremely handsome young proprietor, threading his way towards their table.

'Watch it!' Aileen, who also happened to be sitting the dance out, whispered wryly, conspiratorially. 'It would appear you've caught the eye of our dashing publican, and from what I hear, he's a playboy of the first water.'

'Mmm, so I've been told before,' Rowan smiled. In a relatively small town like the Bay still was, it was impossible to keep anything a secret. 'But what makes you think it's not yourself he's about to chat up?'

'Because I just happen to have been watching him, and he hasn't been able to take his baby blues off you ever since you danced past his table with Jerry. Besides,' her lips twisted crookedly, 'I live here, and he's certainly had enough opportunities before this to—er—further my acquaintance ... if he'd so desired.'

However, although it did prove to be herself Sean chose to address himself to, Rowan still wasn't entirely convinced her friend's supposition had been the correct one for his doing so, and as a result she accepted his ensuing offer to dance somewhat warily.

She half suspected it might have been at Fraser's instigation that Sean had approached her, because even if her boss hadn't been aware of her presence previously, he certainly had been during that particular dance with Jerry which Aileen had mentioned. As she remembered, they'd almost collided with him and Erica as the other pair got up to dance, and the ash-coloured eyes which had locked momentarily with hers—until she'd hastily, selfconsciously, dragged her own gaze away—hadn't exactly been filled with warmth and good cheer. In fact, they'd contained a distinctly sardonic light, she recalled.

Sean drew her closer to avoid a rapidly nearing couple, but conveniently forgot to loosen his hold again once they had passed. 'I've seen you around the Bay a few times, haven't I?' he smiled down at her engagingly.

She had certainly seen him. With his white-blond hair and brilliant blue eyes he stood out in any crowd. 'More than likely,' she granted with a light smile and a shrug. 'I was working at the Shore during the holidays.'

'Ah, the opposition!' He assumed a pained look. 'And now you're working for Fraser, I believe?'

'Mmm.' Then, grasping the bull by the horns, she just had to enquire, no matter how apprehensively, 'Did he suggest you should ask me to dance?'

Sean's brows leapt skywards in obviously genuine amazement. 'Good grief, no!' he half laughed incredulously. 'Believe me, I don't need Fraser to point out the best looking female in the room for me.' Releasing her hand for the moment, he traced the line of her jaw with gentle fingertips, his eyes looking deeply into hers. 'And you are very beautiful, you know.'

Rowan flushed, but refused to take him seriously. 'While you're very smooth,' she returned wryly.

He grinned with such charm that she couldn't help but like him. 'I can tell someone has obviously been maligning my character,' he declared, and sent her a humorously narrowing glance. 'Fraser?'

'Heavens, no! Why would he discuss you with me? I'm only an employee.'

'Then he must be losing his touch, because you'd be more than just an employee if you were on my payroll.' His lips tilted ruefully. 'Why didn't you come to me if you were after work?'

'We did,' she relayed, drily straight-faced. 'Only your manager said you had nothing available.'

'The fool!' he half laughed, half groaned. 'He doesn't know the disservice he's done me when all this time I've just been waiting for the opportunity to meet you.'

Rowan didn't utter a word. She just leant back in his arms and let a highly sceptical glance do her talking for her.

'You don't believe me?' Sean speculated dolefully.

'You're right, I don't believe you,' she chuckled helplessly at the look on his face.

'But we can be friends?'

'I don't see why not,' she acceded, despite the niggling suspicion that occurred to her that Sean Goddard might have been even smoother than she had at first thought.

'Then how about we share a bottle of champagne to celebrate the friendship, hmm?' he proposed, and beginning to dance them towards his own table. 'What could be more amiable than that?'

When a just short of horrified look in the direction they were heading showed Fraser to be cynically watching their progress, Rowan could think of a lot of things she would rather do, and she started to hang back in something akin to panic.

'Oh, really, it's not necessary,' she demurred hurriedly. 'And—and my friends will wonder where I've got to.' Then, as a last resort, when it appeared her objections were to be ignored, 'Besides, I'd rather not, if you must know.'

That at least succeeded in stopping him for a little. 'Why? Don't you like champagne?'

'It's not that. It's just that—well . . .' she chewed at her lip uncomfortably, 'Fraser *is* my boss, and I'm sure I'll feel awkward sitting at the same table with him.' Without a doubt she knew she'd feel that! 'On top of which, I'm hardly dressed for the kind of company you're keeping.' She had already noticed the other two men sharing his table, and their female companions were no less expensively attired than Erica.

'Then if those are your only reasons, you can take it from me, you've got no worries,' he dismissed her arguments with a smile and, to her dismay, started for the table again. 'I've known Fraser too long to believe he wouldn't be anything but approving to have someone as decorative as you around . . . employee or not,' lightly tapping an emphasising forefinger to the end of her daintily retroussé nose. 'As for what you're wearing,' he shrugged offhandedly, 'why should it matter? Even if you wore sackcloth and ashes you'd still outshine every other woman in the room.'

Although his effusive compliments brought a selfconscious colour to her smooth cheeks, they unfortunately didn't put her at her ease, and she was still protesting, 'Oh, but . . .!' when Sean whirled them to a halt beside his friends.

Rowan acknowledged the following introductions stiffly, even though the two businessmen and their wives seemed sociable enough, and took the seat Sean offered between himself and Fraser even less enthusiastically. This was the last place she really wanted to be, and right at that moment, if the floor had opened up and swallowed her she would only have been extremely thankful.

Around her, the others continued their conversation while Sean efficiently uncorked the champagne he had promptly ordered on his return, but apart from a small, 'Thank you,' when a slender-stemmed glass had been filled with the pale gold liquid and handed to her, she sat silently waiting for the chance when she could reasonably, she hoped, make her excuses and leave.

Sean passed round the rest of the glasses, and under cover of the movement, Fraser leant closer to her. 'You're not usually this quiet,' he mocked softly.

'Perhaps I just don't have anything to say,' she shrugged, but refusing to actually turn and look at him.

'Maybe not ... but I sure as hell do! So shall we dance?'

She swallowed convulsively. 'I don't ...'

'Or would you prefer it if we had our little discussion here?'

With everyone, including the disdainful Miss Melville, looking on! Reluctantly, Rowan followed his lead and began to rise. 'How can I refuse when you're so succinctly persuasive?' she muttered resentfully, and finally condescended to glance at him, with direfully flashing eyes, when he laughed.

'Well, that's great!' Sean lamented wryly behind them. 'Before I can even get sat down to have a drink with her, he's stolen my girl!'

'Sorry, old son, but we have things to discuss,' Fraser grinned back at him unrepentantly as he drew Rowan into his arms.

'He probably wants to tell her it's not usually regarded as acceptable behaviour to join your employer's party uninvited,' Erica's carrying voice reached out to them and had Rowan seething in response. As if she would!

'What do you mean . . . uninvited? I . . .'

The remainder of Sean's expostulated reply was lost as they moved away, and Fraser inclined his dark head sardonically. 'It appears you've made quite a hit with Sean.'

'Anyone passable and over the age of eighteen would no doubt make a hit with Sean,' she snapped with unintended sarcasm. She was too apprehensive of his intentions to be concentrating on her own.

'Why accompany him back to the table, then?'

He surely wasn't of the same mind as his haughty girl-friend! 'Because he wouldn't take no for an answer, that's why!' she threw back at him fierily.

'Oh?' One dark brow sloped upwards in an unspoken taunt. 'You mean, in the same way you never willingly do as you're asked?'

'Since you've never yet *asked* me to do anything, how would you know?' she countered on a tart note.

A short bark of humourless laughter issued from his deeply tanned throat. 'You're trying to tell me that, had I *asked* you to remain in the car, you would have done so, instead of risking your damned fool neck by climbing down that cliff in the dark?'

'I—well . . .' Rowan dropped her gaze guiltily. On this occasion he wasn't altogether wrong. 'You should have let me out when I suggested it. I wasn't going to play gooseberry with you and your girl-friend all evening, and—and that's what it sounded as if you meant me to do,' she faltered defensively. 'Anyway,' with a shrug, 'why should you care if I'd fallen? It would just get me out of your hair that much quicker, wouldn't it?'

'Don't talk such bloody rubbish!' he flayed blisteringly. Then, as loud voices and noisy laughter could be heard coming from Rowan's table, he cast a pointed look in that direction and countered her previous remark with a sarcastic, 'And don't tell me that's the kind of company you prefer instead!'

'Oh, Bernie and Damien are all right.' To her annoyance Rowan found herself back on the defensive once again, but refusing to admit she too had sometimes found their exuberant behaviour a little trying, not to say embarrassing. 'As a matter of fact, they're giving me a lift back to the Crossroads,' she disclosed slyly, triumphantly.

The grey of Fraser's eyes darkened appreciably. 'Tonight?' he exploded disparagingly. 'In their condition? Oh, no, they're not!'

'In the morning, as it so happens!' she contradicted pleasurably.

'You think they'll have recovered by then?'

'I've been led to believe so.'

'And in the meantime you're spending the night . . . where?'

'With a friend.' Not that it was any concern of his!

'Male?'

Holding her initial surge of anger at his continued cross-questioning in check, Rowan sent him a mocking glance from beneath thick, glossy lashes. 'And if it is?' she hazarded.

To her surprise, as well as considerable consternation, he smiled lazily, and with such a heart-stopping curve to his firm mouth that she looked away in confusion. Why on earth should he seem to have the ability to make her pulse race when Sean, who was certainly no less attractive—or any of the men from her own crowd, if it came to that—didn't affect it in the slightest?

'Wrong answer—wrong expression, honey,' he bent his head in order to drawl with aggravating astuteness. 'For someone as perversely independent as you, it would have been more in keeping for you to admit it—defiantly . . . if it was true.'

Rowan grimaced sardonically and pounced on the only point she could dispute. 'Just what do you mean . . . *perversely* independent?' she demanded indignantly.

'Well, what else would you call it when you've deliberately arranged this lift for yourself rather than accept my offer?' His brows flicked satirically high.

'You didn't offer exactly,' she parried. 'You merely said I'd no doubt need transport home.'

'Don't split hairs with me, honey,' he warned, his glance a speaking one which had her shrugging uneasily.

'So—so how was I to know you'd still be of the same mind after I'd left your car without—er—permission?'

'I think we've just come full circle,' he declared ironically. 'Because the answer to that is, by not being so contrary as to leave it in the first place.'

'Oh, well, what's done is done, I suppose,' she offered airily. And in a hopeful tone, 'Is that all you wanted to speak to me about?'

Fraser shook his head slowly. 'Not quite. I wanted to *ask*,' with drawling emphasis, 'at what time you proposed moving up to the house tomorrow. In the morning, or the afternoon? As I recall, you never did say.'

The memory of his insistence that it take place tomorrow at all had her automatically choosing the later time. 'In the afternoon, of course.'

'I think it would be better if you did so in the morning.'

No doubt he would! 'By the time I get back from here, I very much doubt there'll be time to do all my packing.'

'Then perhaps you should reconsider about returning tonight, after all,' he suggested subtly.

Oh, no, he wasn't going to catch her that way! 'I'll find time!' she snapped unthinkingly.

'Good. Then I'll send someone down to collect you about eight, shall I?' His eyes locked tauntingly with hers.

Rowan didn't reply. Not because she was wrathfully aware that no acknowledgment on her part was really necessary, but because she was just too irate to form any words at all. So once again he'd managed to get his way in the end! she smouldered impotently. No wonder he and Sean got along so well. They were two of a kind. The worst kind!

CHAPTER FIVE

AFTER two weeks Rowan had more or less become reconciled to living in Fraser's home—at least, on the surface—although not to his increasingly unsettling presence, and she much preferred it when Alice and herself were the only occupants of the house, as now. She could relax with Alice—provided she said nothing detrimental against the master of the house, of course—and she enjoyed working with, as well as learning from, the older woman. This afternoon, when the housekeeper had discovered, to her apparent horror, and Rowan's amusement, that her youthful assistant had never actually baked a cake, apart from one somewhat indigestible effort at school, she had decided it was a circumstance which needed to be immediately rectified and had set about doing so with a will.

Now, as Rowan slid two filled pans into the oven and pushed closed the door, she turned to her mentor to ask, 'How long should they take? Three-quarters of an hour?'

'Good lord, no! You don't need anything like that length of time for a sponge,' Alice advised, giving her lightly greying head a wry shake. 'Didn't your mother teach you anything about baking?'

'No,' Rowan answered shortly, her features visibly tightening, and continued clearing from the table the bowls and utensils she had used.

As she noticed the change, Alice's expression became thoughtful. 'A lack of communication between the two of you, perhaps?' she probed gently.

'I guess you could say that,' Rowan shrugged and half laughed, sardonically.

'So what do your and Tanya's parents think of the two of you moving around the country like you're doing?'

'Tanya's parents are dead. As for mine,' both slender shoulders rose in a carefully offhand gesture, 'I wouldn't know.'

'You don't know how they feel about it?' Alice's eyes widened incredulously.

'I don't know whether they're dead or not,' Rowan revealed flatly, beginning to load the dishwasher.

'You don't know . . .!' Alice came to a gasping halt, looking just plain astounded now. 'I think you'd better leave that,' waving a hand distractedly towards the dishes, 'and come and explain.'

'There's nothing to explain,' denied Rowan with studious calm. 'I never knew one, and the other apparently didn't want to know me, that's all.'

'*All!*' Alice almost choked on the word. 'It seems to me that's an understatement, if ever I've heard one!'

'Not really,' Rowan attempted to smile, only it was too strained to be particularly convincing. She was already regretting having divulged as much as she had. It wasn't a subject she could usually be drawn on at all, and she supposed it was only due to Alice's warm companionship that she'd been so unguardedly forthcoming this time. 'When you've heard that, you've heard just about all there is to tell.' And picking up the flour container from the table, she hurried on, hoping to be diverting, 'If we don't need this any more, I'll put it back in the pantry.'

'It can wait.' Despite being seated, Alice managed to swiftly relieve her of the container and set it down on the table again. 'And so can the rest of these things,' when Rowan showed signs of collecting more for the dishwasher. She indicated a stool not far from her chair. 'You just sit yourself down there for a while and tell your old Aunty Alice all about it, mm? I may not have ever had children of my own, but I do know it often helps to confide your troubles in someone older,' she smiled persuasively.

It was the first time in her life anyone had claimed kinship with Rowan, even of a nominal kind, and it was her undoing. Her eyes began to mist traitorously— something they hadn't done, she hadn't let them do, for years—and she blinked rapidly to dispel the warm dampness before it could betray her by overflowing on to her lashes.

'Wh-what makes you think I—I've got any troubles?' she dissembled shakily, but perching on the stool as she'd been bid. 'I can't remember ever having any parents, so why should a lack of them worry me now?'

'That's what I'm hoping you'll tell me, because I suspect it still does, doesn't it?' Alice deduced shrewdly.

Rowan looked down at her interlaced fingers. 'In a way, I suppose,' she sighed faintly, and still somewhat evasively.

'What way?'

'You're very persistent,' Rowan looked up to half smile wryly.

'I know. It's a trait of mine,' Alice wasn't slow in admitting. 'What way?'

Hunching her shoulders, Rowan then let them fall resignedly. 'I—well, it's difficult to explain really, but I think it's more the reason why, than the actually being without parents that—that . . .'

'Hurts?'

'Something like that, I guess,' she admitted flatly.

'So what is the reason you don't have any?' Alice frowned sympathetically.

'I've already told you. Because . . .'

'I know what you told me,' the older woman cut across her in an ironic tone. 'But that, unfortunately, was somewhat more confusing than enlightening, so I might suggest you start right at the very beginning this time.'

'Right at the beginning? Well, let me see . . .' Rowan pursed her lips meditatively, a protective flippancy entering her voice. 'In the beginning I guess there must have been my father, but since, as far as I can gather, he promptly shot through like the proverbial Bondi tram the moment he discovered he'd carelessly made my mother pregnant, that's about the sum total of my knowledge where he's concerned. My mother, on the other hand, I do know a little more about. Although whether that's a benefit or not, of course, I've never quite been able to decide.' She stopped for a second, her breath coming unevenly, then continued determinedly.

'However, considering she did have me, I suppose I should be grateful for that at least, but by the time I was nine months old the novelty of having a baby was apparently starting to wear off—not to mention being a severe drag on her social life—so when she found another man, willing to marry her this time, even if not to support someone else's bastard, she was more than happy to bundle me off to the nearest children's home where, apart from a number of unsuccessful sojourns in various foster-homes, I spent the next fifteen-odd years of my life.' With a sharply exhaled sigh, she eyed the woman watching her almost challengingly. 'So there you have it. The unabridged version of my life story. Neat, huh?'

A frown of compassion swept over Alice's face. 'Who told you all this?' she questioned intently.

'Matron Willis at the home. She said it was good for the character to know the truth about one's beginnings.'

'Oh, did she! And just how old were you when she decided all that information would do your character good?'

The corners of Rowan's mouth tilted crookedly. Now that the most difficult disclosures had been made, she could begin to relax a little again. 'Around eight or nine, I think. She wasn't very happy with me at the time because I'd just been sent back from about my third foster-home.'

'Why?' Alice's expression changed from one of disgust to one of curiosity.

'Why was I sent back, you mean? Oh, the couple already had two daughters of their own and relations between us weren't exactly as harmonious as they could have been,' Rowan relayed lightly. In actual fact, she remembered, the pair of them had been so jealous of even the smallest amount of attention she'd received that, for once, it had been a relief to be returned to the home.

Alice mulled contemplatively over the information. 'Considering you were only nine months old when you first went there, I'm surprised you hadn't been adopted long before that.'

It was a thought that had often occurred to Rowan herself during the latter years, but when she'd broached the subject with Matron the replies she'd received hadn't been particularly informative. 'Maybe even then I was displaying evidence of my wayward nature—as Matron liked to call it,' she shrugged dismissively. 'She always said that right from the first I'd always had too much to say for myself and wasn't humble enough in view of my lowly station in life.'

'She sounds just the woman to have in charge of a children's home,' commented Alice tartly. 'She certainly didn't intend for you to be overly endowed with self-confidence, did she?'

'No, I suppose not,' Rowan half laughed, half grimaced wryly. 'Although I should point out she wasn't like that just to me, she was like it to all the other kids as well. Even Tanya, when she arrived after her parents were killed, and you couldn't find anyone more self-effacing than Tanya. We used to think Matron was just trying to prepare us for the world of hard knocks, you might say, once we finally left the home. Unfortunately, she just went about it with the delicacy of an ore-crusher, that's all.' Sliding to her feet, she moved towards the oven. 'However, I think that's quite enough about me for one afternoon. Shouldn't these be done by now?'

During the next few minutes, though, as she tested the two nicely risen sponges under Alice's directions and turned them out on to a wire rack to cool, Rowan found her thoughts ungovernably following a similar line, but with regard to someone else entirely.

'Anyway, being parentless doesn't seem to be anything extraordinary round here,' she began as casually as possible. 'What about Evan? Or Fraser, if it comes to that.' Added as if it was an afterthought.

Recovering from her initial surprise, Alice began to laugh. 'But they're not parentless—either of them,' she advised. 'Oh, it's true Fraser's father died quite some years ago, but his mother is still certainly very much alive. These days she's very happily married to a man named Andrew Hampton who runs his own earth-moving business on the Downs in Queensland, but they often come visiting. In fact, they were supposed to have been down this Christmas, but something came up at the last minute and they couldn't make it.'

'I see,' Rowan nodded, but thought she still should enquire, 'And Evan?'

'Ah, yes, Evan,' the housekeeper repeated with a note of fond exasperation in her voice. At least, that was how it sounded to her listener. 'Well, both his parents are still alive. His father—Fraser's uncle—is a stockbroker in Melbourne, but since Evan decided he didn't want to work in the city, Fraser offered him work up here.'

'Which he enjoys, apparently.'

'Yes—well, for a while there it was touch and go,' Alice divulged with a trace of irony. 'Evan's interest was always difficult to hold, and still is in some matters, I'm afraid.' Her eyes sought Rowan's anxiously. 'Your friend isn't expecting anything permanent to eventuate between the two of them, is she?'

She sounded as if she was quoting Fraser, thought Rowan dismally. But as for Tanya . . . 'To be honest, I'm not really sure at the moment,' she confessed lamely. Since she'd moved into the house there had been very few opportunities to discuss the matter with her friend. 'I know she was originally, but—but it's not wholly beyond the bounds of reason that Evan could reciprocate her feelings, is it?'

'No, I suppose not, except . . .'

'Except fickleness happens to be the Delaneys' middle name!' Rowan broke in abrasively.

'I don't understand,' Alice frowned, shaking her head.

Realising she was about to do the unthinkable—criticise Alice's favourite—Rowan determinedly swallowed the knot of apprehension which had lodged in her throat and did it anyway. 'Well, you could hardly call Fraser a model of stability in that regard either, could you?' she charged. 'Whenever he takes a girl out it's a different one just about every time, and even you said you thought he should be married by now.'

'Mmm, I must admit some of what you say is true,' Alice astonished her by conceding. Then her expression altered subtly. 'Although I'm not quite certain just why you should apparently feel so strongly about it.'

Rowan flushed selfconsciously. 'I—I don't, personally,' she denied in a taut voice. 'I was merely speaking on Tanya's behalf, because—because to my mind there doesn't seem to be anything to choose between either of them. Otherwise, why would it matter to me how Fraser conducts his love life?' Her eyes widened innocently.

'One wonders,' mused Alice drily. 'In fact, one tends to wonder quite a few things about you where Fraser's concerned.'

'Oh?' A nervous half smile pulled at Rowan's lips for a moment and then disappeared. 'That sounds intriguing,' she attempted to joke, uneasily.

'I've certainly found it so this last couple of weeks, and especially the way your whole attitude changes the minute he walks into the room. It's very noticeable, you know.'

Which didn't surprise Rowan in the slightest, seeing she was half expecting to be fired most of the time, whether for legitimate reasons or otherwise. Although she doubted Alice would either understand or believe her reasons for thinking that.

'It's probably because I'm not used to living in the same house as my employer,' she offered excusingly instead.

'I see,' the housekeeper nodded wryly. 'So it has nothing to do with your finding him attractive, then?'

'God, no! I mean, no, I don't find him attractive,' Rowan qualified hastily in panic-stricken accents, then promptly modified again, 'Well, he is, of course, but not to me, if you know what I mean.' Frantically she cast about for a diversion and chanced upon the very solution. 'Oh, heavens, look at the time!' she exclaimed, and immediately began edging towards the doorway. 'I'm supposed to clean out the offices this afternoon, but I won't have them finished before dinner if I don't get a move on. I'm sorry to leave in such a rush, but I'll be back as quickly as I can.'

'After you've had time to think over what I said, hmm?' quipped Alice banteringly.

The colour in Rowan's cheeks heightened markedly. 'There's no need to. I—I've already explained my thoughts on that,' she alleged, albeit somewhat shakily, and hurried out through the flyscreen door.

Well, naturally she hadn't wanted to listen to any more of Alice's idle speculations, she reasoned defensively as she made her way across to the office building. Apart from being embarrassing, they were also completely without foundation! She couldn't possibly be attracted to someone who seemed so arrogantly determined to run her private life for her.

Then why was he so often in her thoughts, and why should the memory of his warm mouth possessing hers still have such an unsettling effect on her? questioned an insidious voice from the deeper recesses of her mind. One, because she hated being so completely under his control, and the other, because she'd been totally unprepared for such an occurrence, she rationalised plausibly, conveniently. And the effortless way in which he started her heart pounding at times? the voice aggravatingly refused to be silenced. With an impatient toss of her head which set her long blonde ponytail swinging, Rowan declined to search very deeply for an answer. It was disconcerting enough just knowing it happened, without looking for causes!

Hazel Baxter, Fraser's recently married secretary, was at her desk in the reception area when Rowan walked in, and after quickly ascertaining that their boss was absent for the moment, she hurried around the outer corridor to the store room where the cleaning gear was kept before the other girl had a chance to add anything further—as it appeared she had intended. There wasn't time for them to have a chat this afternoon and Rowan was all too anxious to have Fraser's office finished before he returned.

With a duster in one hand and pulling a vacuum cleaner behind her with the other, she knocked perfunctorily on the door of the main office and walked straight in—only to have surprise halting her in her tracks at the sight of Erica Melville comfortably ensconced in one of the padded leather visitor's chairs. Dressed today in a severely tailored, but extremely becoming, black and white slacks suit, and with not a strand of her intricately styled hair out of place, the haughty redhead made Rowan's faded jeans and loosely fitting cotton shirt appear even older than they were, and no one was more conscious of the fact than their wearer, even if they were the most suitable clothes for the work she was doing.

'Good afternoon,' she finally acknowledged formally, advancing a little further into the room. Now she knew what Hazel had been going to tell her! 'I'm sorry, but I didn't realise you were in here. I was going to clean . . .'

'Well, don't let me stop you,' Erica interrupted in a bored voice, flicking the ash from the cigarette held between immaculately manicured fingers in the general direction of the ashtray on Fraser's desk but missing it completely. 'It looks as if the place could do with it.'

With her making such a mess, Rowan didn't doubt it, but seeing she could hardly say as much, she merely shrugged and got on with what she had to do.

For a time Erica watched her absently, her fingers drumming a restless tattoo on the desk top, then after she had carelessly dropped the still glowing butt of her cigarette in the ashtray and almost immediately lit another, her lips curved into a sardonic line and her green gaze sharpened spitefully.

'I suppose for someone like you, cleaning is a step up after working in a factory, isn't it?' she derided.

Rowan inhaled deeply, steadyingly, and continued dusting the bookshelves behind the desk. 'It has its compensations,' she allowed stiffly. Actually, it gave her quite a deal of pleasure when there were such beautiful objects to care for, as in the Delaney household.

'Like . . . keeping you under the boss's nose?'

It was so far from the truth that Rowan couldn't conceal her amazement. 'That's the last thing I want!' she ejaculated with feeling.

'Oh, don't try giving me that!' Erica spat, and obviously disbelieving. 'You made it pathetically clear just what you were angling for when you had yourself invited to Fraser's table the other night at the Bay.'

'Then if it was so pathetic, I can't see why you

should be in such a flap about it now,' Rowan promptly retorted.

'Because it was extremely embarrassing for the rest of us seeing you make such a fool of yourself! Fraser's never likely to be interested in someone of your kind, and the sooner you're made to realise that the better it will be for you, as well as everyone else!' She gave a derogatory laugh. 'Good lord, one look around the table should have convinced you just how out of place you were that evening, and hanging on here isn't going to do you any good either. So if I were you I'd move on very swiftly ... before Fraser is forced to tell you himself how irritating your presence is becoming.'

Rowan only wished she could move on, and as for Fraser finding her presence irritating ... well, she'd known that right from the beginning, even though it was for different reasons than Erica imagined. However, the older woman's malicious remarks hadn't been exactly endearing or necessary, to her mind, and in consequence she had absolutely no intention of telling her just how surprisingly attuned their thoughts really were.

'Yes, well, thanks for the advice,' she murmured, drily tongue-in-cheek.

'You're going to do as I suggest?' Erica could hardly keep the eagerness out of her voice.

Rowan lifted the ashtray from the desk and casually flicked the remaining ash away, mostly towards the redhead on the opposite side. 'Oh, I shouldn't think so,' she replied ingenuously. 'And especially not while Alice is still incapacitated. That wouldn't really be fair to her at all.'

Erica's eyes blazed furiously. 'As if you give a damn about Alice! And watch where you're putting that ash, can't you?' She brushed frantically at her slacks suit.

'I'm so sorry.' Rowan bit at her lip in mock contrition and, replacing the ashtray, dropped the duster on the desk and hurried around to the vacuum cleaner. 'Here, this will get it all off you,' she declared, turning the machine on, and extending the foot towards the other girl.

'For God's sake, get that thing away from me! It's probably filthy after being all over the floor!' squealed Erica in outrage. 'And don't think you've outsmarted me either, you transparent little bitch, because I'm wide awake to your tricks, I can tell you!'

'How very perspicacious of you!' quipped Rowan facetiously and, deciding against completing the dusting, continued vacuuming instead. She could always return tomorrow and finish the other—when Erica wasn't there!

While the cleaner was going at least there was a respite from Erica's barbed tongue, Rowan discovered thankfully, although that was no inducement to take any longer than was absolutely necessary, and in the end it was very much a lick and a promise that the room received. A fact which apparently didn't escape a malevolent pair of green eyes either, for immediately the machine was switched off the redhead had words to say on the subject.

'You surely don't think you've finished, do you?' she jeered in incredulous tones.

Not that it was any of her business, but ... 'For today, yes,' was the curt confirmation.

'That's what you think, my girl!' Erica contradicted in her most patronising voice. 'Now you get on and do it to my satisfaction or I'll be having something to say to Fraser about your standard of work!'

Her tone, as much as her words, had Rowan's ire

rising uncontrollably. 'Like blazes I'll do anything to *your* satisfaction!' she seethed. 'You're not my employer, you're just a visitor here, and I'm damned if I'll have you telling me what to do!'

'How dare you call me *just* a visitor!' Erica shrilled, leaping to her feet in a rage. 'And in Fraser's absence you'll do as I say, you . . .!'

'You'll be lucky!' Rowan cut in to gibe sarcastically.

'Luckier than you expect when I get through . . .!'

'What the hell is going on here?' A livid male voice interrupted the older woman's tirade this time as, unnoticed by either of them, Fraser entered the room to stand with his hands resting on lean hips, his silver-grey eyes snapping ominously as they encompassed the two bristling figures before him.

'Oh, thank goodness you're back!' Erica recovered first to sigh dramatically as she sank back into her chair. Her eyes glittered glacially as they swept over the younger girl. 'You can have absolutely no idea just how unco-operative and insolent this—this girl has been during your absence.'

'Oh?' If possible, Fraser's gaze hardened as it came to rest on Rowan's defiantly challenging face.

Erica was only too pleased to elucidate. 'Mmm, apart from deliberately brushing all the dust in my direction, just because I remarked on her standard of work, or rather lack thereof—I mean, you could hardly call that clean, could you?' pointing to the area around her chair where, to Rowan's vexation, she could see the carpet which had been cleaned was now indiscriminately, and undoubtedly purposely, littered with ash from Erica's last cigarette, 'she said she didn't plan to do it any better, and that she certainly wouldn't be doing anything to *my* satisfaction.'

A muscle flickered momentarily beside Fraser's

levelling mouth. 'Is that true?' he demanded harshly
of Rowan.

For her part, Rowan gave him back a look as
condemning as his own. 'Would you believe me if I
said it wasn't?' she countered ironically.

'Well, is it?'

She shrugged defeatedly. 'More or less, I suppose.'
What would be the point in trying to explain? He
wasn't likely to be interested in her side of the story,
and especially not when his girl-friend—one of his
numerous girl-friends, she added acidly—was doing
her best to present the matter in the most damning
way possible.

'Then you'd better apologise, hadn't you?' he
proposed tersely as he moved past her, making for the
swivel chair behind the desk.

Apologise! To Erica? After the manner in which
she'd set out to create friction? Never! Taking a deep
breath, Rowan avoided looking at the older woman's
triumphantly smirking face and replied on a low, taut
note, 'No!'

'You see, I told you she was unco-operative and
insolent!' Erica promptly accused, but at least giving
Rowan the satisfaction of seeing that irritatingly smug
expression wiped off her face.

From behind the desk, Fraser looked up sharply. 'If
you don't, you realise what the consequences will be,
don't you?'

'She'll be dismissed, I should hope!' put in Erica
optimistically.

The other two ignored her, although Rowan was
only too aware that that was exactly what he was
suggesting, and she chewed at her lower lip worriedly.
Not even for Tanya could she apologise to the
malicious Erica Melville, she just couldn't! But nor

could she bear the thought of the woman witnessing her dismissal, and so she made the only decision she could that would allow her to retain at least a little of her pride.

'I'll save you the bother,' she told Fraser in a determinedly careless tone, her head held rebelliously high. 'I just quit.'

'The first correct thing she's done all afternoon,' Erica couldn't resist crowing.

To Rowan's surprise, however, Fraser didn't appear anywhere near as satisfied with her decision as she'd anticipated, for his demeanour didn't alter one iota from its previous narrow-eyed aspect.

'In that case, I guess there's nothing more to be said, then,' he accepted her resolve in a brusque fashion. 'I'll see you afterwards about . . .'

The sudden ringing of the telephone on his desk brought him to a halt and as he picked it up Rowan began collecting the cleaning equipment, preparing to leave. Behind her she heard him answer, then apologise with marked sarcasm, and could hardly believe her ears when he advised in a biting tone, 'It's for you, Rowan.'

'M-me?' she stammered, turning to stare almost disbelievingly at him.

'Mmm. It's Sean.' His mouth formed a grim, tight line as he held out the receiver towards her.

'Oh!' Her eyes widened in astonishment, wondering what he could want. 'I—I'll take it outside,' she offered, taking an agitated step in that direction.

'He's already through to this phone,' impatiently. 'Apparently Hazel automatically thought he wanted me and put him through without giving him the chance to say it was you he wanted to speak to.'

'I see,' Rowan acknowledged weakly, and reluctantly

relieved him of the receiver. She supposed he was annoyed, and rightly so, she granted, at a private call being taken in his office, but she was certainly no more in favour of the idea than he was! Selfconsciously, she put the phone to her ear and half turned away, not wanting to actually turn her back on him, but at the same time not wanting to face him, or Erica, either.

'Hello . . . Sean?'

'Sure is, beautiful,' came the reply together with a disarming laugh. 'What took you so long?'

'Oh, I—er . . .' She stopped discomfitedly, aware that the other two in the room could hear every word spoken, and decided against attempting to explain. 'What did you want to talk to me about?'

'The dinner-dance in the Palm Garden this evening,' he enlightened her swiftly. 'I'm hoping you might like to join us?'

'Us?' she queried warily with an instinctive, surreptitious glance at Fraser.

'That's right. Fraser and Erica will be there, plus the Alfords and the Waites. You remember, the two couples you met the other night? Oh, and I believe Evan and your girl-friend are also coming, as well as a whole crowd of others.' His voice lowered persuasively. 'You'll enjoy yourself, I can promise you, beautiful, and it will be the perfect opportunity for you and me to get to know each other better.'

Rowan's lips shaped ruefully. She wasn't at all sure it would be safe to know him any better. 'Yes—well, I appreciate your asking me to the dance, Sean, but I'm sorry . . .'

'Now you're not going to refuse,' he forestalled her hastily with a laugh. 'I won't let you, because I never take no for an answer.'

Something she already knew! 'Except I'm afraid

you're going to have to this time, because I'm already going somewhere this evening.'

'To that beach party Aileen Hughes is arranging?'

He sounded disparaging and she took exception to it. 'As a matter of fact, yes.' And until a few moments ago the place she had believed Tanya and Evan to be going to.

The cooling note in her tone must have got through to him, because his reaction was immediate. 'Look, don't get me wrong, I've got nothing against beach parties—except I'd prefer their custom at the Kurrawa Bay, of course,' he attached a wryly humorous proviso. 'I just think you'll find it more enjoyable at the Palm Garden, that's all—I know I will if you're there—and you can go to a beach party any old time, can't you?'

'Maybe,' she conceded grudgingly. 'But I've still promised Aileen I'd go, and I don't like to break promises. Perhaps some other time.'

'You're not really turning me down, are you?' he lamented plaintively.

From behind her there came a long-suffering sigh—Erica, she surmised—although another covert glance showed Fraser to be looking no less tolerant, and rubbing her free hand nervously down the side of her jeans, she answered Sean rather more abruptly than she intended.

'Yes, I am, I'm sorry. And really, I must be going.'

'Why the panic? That's Fraser's office you're in, isn't it?'

'Precisely!'

'Oh, but he won't mind. We're mates from way back.'

'*You* might be ... *I* definitely am not!' Rowan grimaced expressively. 'And now, I'm sorry, but . . .'

'Hey! What was that supposed to imply?' he cut in curiously.

Rowan didn't pretend not to know what he was referring to, and she gave a strained, but she hoped dismissing, half laugh. 'Nothing much. I'll see you later, Sean.'

'Later this evening, I hope you mean.' He was nothing if not persistent.

'No, that's not what . . .'

Without warning she discovered a strong brown hand relieving her of the phone in mid-sentence and Fraser taking over the conversation. 'Sorry, old son, but this does happen to be a business phone and I'm waiting on an important call, so I'd appreciate it if you'd please get off the line,' he requested in a chafing drawl.

Embarrassed even further by having her disastrously timed call forcibly curtailed, Rowan hurriedly disconnected the vacuum cleaner and headed with it towards the door. With her hand beginning to turn the handle, and hearing Fraser finally replace the receiver, she still had to about-face, though, her lips pressing together apprehensively.

'Yes?' Dusky-framed eyes noted her action coolly.

'I was w-wondering about Tanya,' she faltered, painfully conscious of having put her friend's job in jeopardy.

'Well, what about her?'

Rowan moved uncomfortably from one foot to the other and tried to disregard Erica's obviously interested glance. 'You—er—said that if either of us . . .' She paused, unwilling to discuss it in front of the other woman.

'I know what I said,' Fraser retorted roughly, alleviating her need to go any further, although she doubted that had been the reason for his comment.

'And?' Anxiety had her holding her breath and he took so long considering the matter that her eyes began to cloud with despair.

'I'll think about it!' he snapped at last.

'Thank you,' she sighed in relief, and reached for the door handle again.

'By the way . . .' Before she could open the door fully Fraser's voice sounded behind her once more. 'Do I understand from what you had to say on the phone that you're going to the Bay tonight?'

She spared him a wary glance over one shoulder, not knowing quite why he should have been asking. 'Yes, that's right.'

'By what transport?'

So that was what he was getting at! she fumed. Even though she wasn't in his employ any longer, he still seemed to think he had the right to control her mode of travel. Well, he couldn't have been more wrong!

'That is once again my concern, Fraser . . . and *mine* only!' she derived no little pleasure from being able to smile mockingly before stepping into the corridor and closing the door between them.

CHAPTER SIX

AFTER some long, and at times, awkward minutes spent explaining to Alice approximately what had occurred in the office, Rowan was once more on the telephone—this time to Tanya, who by then had finished work for the day and was back at the Raymonds' house.

'Rowan! What a coincidence!' her friend exclaimed on coming to the phone. 'I was just about to ring you.'

'Regarding your change of plans for this evening?'

'Well, yes, but how did you know?' Surprise was evident in Tanya's voice.

'Oh, word gets around,' replied Rowan wryly, vaguely. 'So it's true, then, is it?'

'That Evan and I are going to the Palm Garden instead of the beach party? Mmm, we thought we might. You don't mind, do you?' Tanya queried anxiously. 'We'll still be able to give you a lift down if you want one, of course.'

She needed one more than ever now, since she'd be taking her belongings with her. There wasn't much to be gained by boarding with Mrs Raymond again when Fraser was the only employer of any note around the Crossroads. She would just have to try her luck at the Bay once more.

'Or why don't you change your mind too and come with us to the Palm Garden?' Tanya went on to suggest enthusiastically.

'No, thanks,' Rowan declined with a rueful half laugh. And, knowing it had to be mentioned some time, 'I haven't the slightest desire to spend the evening in company with my ex-employer.'

'Your *what*!' Tanya almost jumped down the phone at her. 'Oh, Rowan, you're not really referring to Fraser, are you?'

'Sorry, none other.'

'He actually fired you?' It was obvious Tanya was extremely reluctant to believe what she was hearing, and Rowan could understand why.

'Not exactly, I quit . . . to save him the trouble,' was the sardonic disclosure.

'But—but why?' Followed by an audible gasp. 'Oh, I suppose that means I'm out of work now too, doesn't it?'

Thankful she had at least one piece of good news to pass on, Rowan reassured the other girl swiftly. 'No, not yet you're not. I did—er—mention that, but all he said was that he'd think about it. So unless you hear anything to the contrary I presume you're to be allowed to continue working for Evan.'

Tanya's ensuing sigh of relief was as distinct as her prior gasp of dismay had been. 'I'm so glad,' she confessed honestly. 'Although it is rather strange that Fraser didn't insist on me leaving as well, isn't it? I wonder if he's had a change of heart concerning Evan and myself. Do you think that's what it could be?'

Privately, Rowan doubted it, but then whoever knew just what went on inside Fraser's head? She'd expected him to be jumping for joy this afternoon at the thought of her leaving, and yet that certainly hadn't been the impression he'd given. For her friend's sake, though, she was prepared to be a little less dubious.

'It could be, I guess,' she conceded. 'In any event, you'll probably have a better idea regarding that after tonight, seeing you'll be spending the evening with him, I expect.'

'Hmm, except that's not really the most important matter at the moment. What is, is what you're going to do now.' Tanya returned to their most pressing problem. 'And nor have you yet explained why you resigned in the first place.'

Rowan enlightened her as briefly as possible, both with regard to the happenings in the office and her plan to again seek work in Kurrawa Bay.

'Well, if that's what happened I don't blame you for resigning rather than apologising,' Tanya supported her decision loyally. 'But do you really think you'll be able to find employment at the Bay? I mean, we did try every avenue there before.'

'Something could have come up in the meantime, though,' Rowan suggested. It was feasible, but even if it didn't prove to be the case, she did have another string of sorts to her bow these days. Not that she intended mentioning it to anyone, not even Tanya, or that she would be using it if it came to that, but as a last resort she supposed there was always Sean to be considered. At the cabaret he had all but said he would have found them work if he'd known they were looking, so perhaps if nothing else eventuated she might have no other choice but to see if he was as good as his word.

'Or maybe Evan will be able to think of something again,' proposed Tanya. 'I'll ask him on the quiet this evening.'

'All help gratefully received,' Rowan quipped, then swallowed involuntarily as she looked out of the window to see a familiar figure approaching the house with loose-limbed strides. 'Meanwhile, I see someone coming I'd rather avoid at present, so we'll have to continue this later, okay?'

'Sure. I'll see you when Evan calls for me.'

Uttering a hasty goodbye, Rowan replaced the receiver in its cradle and hurrying up the stairs, as quickly as she could, made it to her room before Fraser even entered the house. Despite her unconcerned attitude while talking to Tanya, inwardly she was finding the prospect of leaving strangely unattractive, but rather than give Fraser an opportunity to guess at the state of her disconcerting feelings, she preferred to keep well out of his path altogether.

As it turned out, by the time Evan knocked on her door a couple of hours later to advise they ought to be leaving, she hadn't seen Fraser again at all, although she deduced that he must have told the younger man what had occurred because, apart from a mild surprise to see her taking her luggage with her, he accepted the situation philosophically.

At the bottom of the stairs, Evan immediately turned for the front door, but Rowan hesitated for a moment. 'I won't be long, but I would like to say goodbye to Alice,' she half smiled apologetically.

He nodded his understanding. 'I know Alice would like you to too. You go ahead, I'll wait for you in the car.'

'Thanks, Evan.' The words were no sooner out than she was rushing along the hall towards the housekeeper's two rooms which, for convenience, were on the ground floor.

'I just came to say goodbye,' she smiled faintly at the older woman after being invited inside the neat sitting room.

Alice patted her arm comfortingly. 'That was very thoughtful of you, but you just concentrate on enjoying yourself and forget about your worries for a while, hmm? I'll look forward to seeing you in the morning and hearing all about it.'

Abruptly realising that the housekeeper had misconstrued her meaning, Rowan's smile faded. 'I meant, goodbye for always, Alice,' she clarified sadly. 'I won't be coming back.'

'Not coming back?' Alice stared at her in disbelief. 'But of course you will! Just because you've resigned it doesn't mean you have to leave immediately, and I'm positive Fraser doesn't expect you to. You wait here while I call him, because I know he'll tell you the same.'

'No! Please, Alice!' Rowan caught at her arm in a panic to stop her. 'I—I'd rather it this way, although I am sorry to be leaving you in the lurch without a helper.'

'Oh, that's not so important,' Alice disclaimed negligently. 'Even though I shall miss you. I've become quite used to having you around, and certainly no one could have cared for the place more. Are you sure you have to leave tonight?'

Rowan nodded, a desolate lump lodging in her throat. 'I shall miss you too, Alice. You're the most understanding person I've ever known,' she confessed huskily, and on impulse bent to kiss the woman's soft cheek before whirling through the doorway and running down the hall. If she wasn't careful she would soon be making a fool of herself by crying, and that was something she hadn't done since the day Matron had told her why she was in the children's home.

Not surprisingly, the conversation in Evan's car was somewhat subdued on the journey to the Bay, although all three had managed to raise a smile at the difference in their appearances, for whereas Rowan had chosen to wear an old pair of frayed shorts made from cut-down jeans and a halter-necked bikini top for the beach party, Tanya and Evan were dressed rather more formally for their evening at the Palm Garden.

'Will it be okay to leave my luggage in the car, Evan, until I've made arrangements for somewhere to stay tonight?' Rowan enquired as he eventually brought the vehicle to a halt on the Esplanade and she prepared to alight.

'Oh, sure,' he agreed equably. 'Just give us a yell if you want it before the dance finishes and I'll unlock the car for you, or otherwise we'll meet you in the hotel car park afterwards and you can get it then.'

Thanking him, she stepped out on to the footpath and closed the door behind her. 'Well, have a good night, and I'll see you later,' she smiled at them both.

'You too,' reciprocated Tanya. 'Although I do wish you were coming with us.'

Rowan merely looked at her, graphically.

'No, I suppose not, in the circumstances.' Her friend gave a rueful half laugh.

With Tanya and Evan's departure, Rowan set about finding exactly where her own party was to be held—Aileen had only said somewhere on the beach—and then experienced a sinking feeling in the pit of her stomach on seeing the site Aileen had selected. It was barely a hundred metres away from where the Palm Garden met the edge of the sand.

'Whatever made you choose this particular spot?' she couldn't help grimacing as she located the dark-haired organiser among the gathering crowd of young locals and visitors.

'So we could share their lights,' Aileen disclosed with a grin. She looked towards the Garden with its swaying palms and flowering shrubs, the glass-topped aluminium lace tables between sparkling beneath a profusion of coloured lanterns. 'They're having a do there tonight, so I thought it would save us having to provide any illumination. It looks pretty swish, don't you think?'

'Mmm, very,' Rowan allowed, grudgingly. 'Although I don't know if Sean is going to be too happy having us on his doorstep almost.' Nor his patrons either, she surmised. There were couples dancing on the patio outside the hotel, while others were beginning to make their way to the tables, and some of the latter were already casting somewhat disdainful glances towards the group on the beach.

'Whether he is or not, there's nothing he can do about it,' Aileen shrugged. 'We're as entitled to use this section of the beach as any other.'

Rowan didn't comment. In fact, it was doubtful if she even heard because, much to her annoyance, both her attention and her gaze were lingering waywardly on the increasing number of people filling the Garden. That was, until she caught sight of a particularly tall, broad-shouldered form, whereupon with a roughly indrawn breath she averted her gaze rapidly, determinedly, and joined in the preparations for the barbecue with a restless energy that no amount of action seemed able to dissipate.

After the meal was concluded someone produced a guitar and, coupled with the music coming from the hotel, it provided them with a good background for at least some form of dancing, but although Rowan never lacked for partners she couldn't quite summon up her usual spontaneity for such gatherings, and as the night wore on she found she was having to force what little enthusiasm she could muster as her errant glance kept straying more and more often to the brightly lit scene on the grassed terrace slightly above them.

It was on one such occasion that she noticed a male figure stepping from the Garden on to the sand, his distinctive ash-blond hair proclaiming his identity, and she watched curiously as he paced purposely towards the laughing, chattering throng spread over the beach. He appeared to be looking for someone as his blue eyes scanned those dancing, and after a moment's hesitation Rowan separated herself from the group she was with and walked over to him.

'Did you want someone in particular, Sean?' she queried helpfully.

His frowning look of concentration cleared immediately as he saw her and was replaced by an engaging smile. 'You, naturally,' he declared, and dropping an arm about her shoulders began drawing her away to a quieter area.

Rowan went along with him acquiescently, but couldn't restrain a smile as he trudged uncomfortably beside her. 'Your shoes are going to be filled with sand, you know,' she half laughed expressively, and thankful for her own bare feet.

'You're so right!' His grimacing return was no less explicit. 'But it just goes to prove what I'm prepared to suffer for a sight of you.'

'And you're so polished, you're slippery, Sean Goddard!' she charged, drily humorous. It was impossible for her to take Sean's compliments seriously. 'Now what did you want to see me about?'

His lips twitched ruefully. 'You just refuse to believe I'm sincere, don't you?' he countered instead of answering.

'Mmm, I'm afraid I do.'

'For that, I've a good mind not to tell you what I came for at all.' He eyed her mock-threateningly.

'I'm sorry, Sean,' she apologised promptly, but with an uncontrollable chuckle. 'Even if I can't bring myself to believe half of what you say, at least you make me laugh.'

'Oh, great!' His eyes rolled skywards. 'Here I am trying to convince you of my enamoured state, and all you can say is, I make you laugh!' He shook his head in feigned reproof. 'You really don't deserve to hear my news, you know.'

'No, I probably don't,' Rowan conceded with a remorseful half smile. 'But I do have rather a lot on my mind tonight, so maybe . . .'

'And that's why I'm here right now,' he broke in, his arm tightening about her encouragingly. 'I just heard you were looking for work again, and I'm here to offer you a job . . . if you want it.'

'Do I?' she gasped fervently.

'You're interested, then?'

'If you really mean it, very much so,' she nodded.

'Of course I mean it,' he asserted, then glanced down at his sand-covered shoes in disgust. 'Would I go through this if I didn't?'

Rowan laughed in her relief. It was a considerable weight off her mind to know she'd found employment. 'What type of work does it entail?' she enquired interestedly.

'Oh—er—it'll be something of what you'd call a roving commission, I suppose. You know, wherever a hand's needed at the time.' From the hotel came the sound of someone calling his name, and with a crooked grin he tilted her face up to his and lightly kissed her unsuspecting lips. 'I'm sorry, but it seems I'm wanted,' he grimaced. 'Come and see me tomorrow, though, and we'll work something out. Okay?'

Rowan nodded and watched his departure with thoughtful eyes. It had sounded as if Sean intended creating a position solely for her rather than there actually being one available, and she found the idea vaguely disturbing. She wanted legitimate work, not him doing her any special favours, and especially not if he expected her to accept his advances in repayment—as that parting kiss might have suggested. Of course it was possible he didn't want anything in return for his assistance, and that she was doing him an injustice by even thinking he did, but somehow a little of her pleasure at having been offered work seemed to have disappeared all the same.

By now, Sean had reached the Garden and Rowan's gaze continued following his progress absently; seeing him stop for a word with the man who had apparently called to him, and then finally moving along to his own table where he leant down to say something to Fraser before resuming his seat. Whatever he said, it was enough to have his friend's head turning swiftly in Rowan's direction, and suddenly deducing that the lights which presented such a clear view of the hotel patrons were probably outlining herself just as plainly, she promptly spun about and headed for the shadowed water's edge, deciding to go for a walk. At the moment she didn't feel much like forcing herself to display an enthusiasm she was far from experiencing for the dancing, or the inconsequential chatter that was taking place behind her.

Deep in thought, Rowan took her time as she walked, stopping now and again to toss pieces of driftwood into the foaming breakers, and allowing the incoming waves to surge creamily up to her knees. However, it wasn't until she noticed she was almost to Fraser's beach house that she realised just how far she had come, and she would have turned back immediately if something totally unexpected about the house hadn't brought a puzzled and somewhat suspicious crease to her brow. The lights were on!

Undecided whether she should investigate or not, Rowan hovered near the water for a time, then, with a sigh, came to the reluctant conclusion that she should at least take a look. After all, even if she wasn't feeling particularly well disposed towards Fraser, common decency demanded she should make some effort to discover what was happening when she knew both he and Evan were at the hotel in town. Keeping to the shadows, she began moving across the intervening sand carefully, her eyes watchful as they strained for a glimpse of someone passing the windows, or even outside the house if it came to that. Whoever had turned the power on could have been anywhere.

Slowly she inched her way closer to the perimeter of the light spilling across the verandah and on to the sand, then darted on silent feet under the rail and over the wooden boards to flatten herself against the wall before nervously peering through the nearest window. It was the kitchen, but although that particular room was empty, by way of the open doorway leading to the sitting room she could just make out someone's indistinct shadow on the far wall as they crossed behind a table lamp, and she padded towards the room's glass doors in order to get a better view. By the time she reached them, though, the person inside had disappeared, and nervous of being discovered herself, she scurried off the verandah and back to the concealing darkness again.

Not knowing quite what to do now, she finally decided to move back to the other side of the house—apart from the sitting room there were no other lighted rooms on the side she was facing at present—but before she could manage to take more than a few steps a frighteningly heavy hand, made all the more alarming because of the unexpectedness with which it came in the dim light, caught her shoulder from behind.

'Okay, just what the bloody hell do you think you're up to?' rasped a suspicious male voice as she was hauled around roughly to face him.

Rowan almost collapsed with shock. *'Fraser!'* she all but squealed in a mixture of surprise, relief, and anger.

'Rowan?' His tone was no less disbelieving, although he was the first to recover. 'What are you doing creeping around the house?' His silver-grey eyes held hers intently.

She bridled at the still suspicious note she could detect in his voice. 'Well, I wasn't spying on you, if that's what you're thinking! I didn't even know it was you in the house. I thought you were still back at the hotel.'

'Then who did you think it was?'

'I didn't know—that's why I was looking!' she flared. 'It could have been someone who'd broken in, or—or anything!'

Abruptly, his teeth gleamed in such a lazily attractive smile that Rowan felt her breath catching involuntarily in her throat. 'You were protecting *my* property?'

'I—I would have done the same for anyone,' she alleged with a shrug, annoyed with herself both for letting him disturb her so adolescently, and for having revealed too much.

'Anyone *else* . . . maybe,' he drawled.

It was said with a teasing inflection Rowan was

neither prepared for, nor knew how to combat, and in consequence she sought to protect herself by deliberately misunderstanding him. 'In other words, you still don't believe me, is that it?' Then, without giving him time to reply, she shrugged, and continued with apparent insouciance, 'Well, that's up to you, of course. I wouldn't expect you to take my word for anything,' with a touch of resentment. 'But in any event, I think I'd better be getting back now. I didn't intend to be away for all that long.' She pulled away from his now slackened grasp.

'Uh-uh, to all of those,' he vetoed immediately, recapturing her by the wrist. 'You and I have some talking to do, and now's as good a time as any, I guess.'

'What, with Erica adding her two cents' worth again?' she burst out hotly, scornfully, and gesturing towards the house with her free hand. She couldn't imagine the redhead had allowed him to leave without her and therefore presumed she was inside.

Fraser shook his head slowly, his mouth curving obliquely. 'No, just the two of us. I seem to have more success that way.'

'Oh, I don't know,' she mocked. 'I would have thought she'd given you your biggest success yet by getting rid of me this afternoon.'

'Except that when I dismiss any of my staff . . .'

'You didn't dismiss me, I resigned!' she interposed indignantly.

'Don't quibble,' he admonished with a sardonic half smile. 'You know as well as I do that you only preempted my intention by mere seconds.'

'You still didn't fire me!' Her dark eyes flashed with a mutinous light. In view of the circumstances, the point was an especially important one to her.

'All right ... when any of my staff resign,' he relented unexpectedly and altered his wording, 'I prefer to be in possession of *all* the facts, not just a few of them.' He tilted her face up to his. 'Why didn't you tell me Erica had been unpleasant from the time you entered the room?'

'Who told you she had?' Rowan was more interested in asking. She doubted Erica herself would have volunteered such a confession.

'Hazel. Apparently the intercom was on and she heard everything that was said.'

'I see,' she nodded. 'But if I hadn't happened to come along here tonight, you wouldn't have told me you knew the truth, I suppose?'

His brows snapped together in a frown. 'What makes you think that?'

'It's obvious, isn't it? You had plenty of time to mention it before I left the house,' she paused, eyeing him bitterly, 'but you didn't, did you?'

'Mainly because I just wasn't expecting you to take to your heels quite so hurriedly, or so secretly!' he retorted in caustic tones. 'In fact, I had no idea you weren't still in the house until Alice came to tell me ... almost in tears, I might add!'

Rowan dropped her gaze uncomfortably. 'Yes, well, I'm sorry for that,' she murmured miserably. She hadn't wanted to cause the housekeeper any distress. 'I didn't like leaving her without an assistant.'

'That wasn't why she was upset! But if you didn't like doing it, then why do so?'

'Because I thought that was better than—than ...' She faltered to a halt and began irritably trying to tug her arm free. 'Oh, what does it matter? You've got what you've always wanted, so who cares?'

'Seemingly Alice, for one.' His voice gentled even if his grip didn't. 'And leaving was better than . . . what, Rowan?' he probed insistently.

Her toes curled deeply into the sand. 'Being told to get out,' she sighed.

'But Alice told you you wouldn't be expected to leave immediately.'

'Mmm, but then Alice wasn't aware you were just sweating on a reason, any reason, to fire me, was she?' Her eyes widened sarcastically.

'Nor was I,' he partly drawled, partly laughed.

'Not much you weren't! You know damned well that's been your prime objective ever since you were forced into reluctantly hiring us!' she stormed resentfully. Then, hunching one shoulder, she simmered down somewhat. 'Not that it matters now, anyway. I've found work elsewhere.'

'With Sean?' He gave a full-throated but rather mocking laugh this time.

'And what's wrong with that?' she demanded indignantly. 'I thought he was a friend of yours.'

'He is,' came the exceedingly dry concurrence. 'That's how come I know the way he works.'

'Meaning?'

Lively grey eyes fixed her with a humorously taunting glance. 'Oh, come on, honey, I thought you once told me you knew your way around. What do you think I mean?'

Rowan dismally suspected the same as had occurred to her, although she was loath to admit as much. 'You're only saying that because you don't want him to employ me!' she accused.

'You don't think I could have stopped him offering you any work, if that was my intention?' His brows peaked expressively.

'You may have tried to, and been unsuccessful, for all I know.'

'And you're refusing to accept the obvious! So tell me, just what position did he offer you?'

'That's none of your business!' she parried discomfitedly.

His shapely mouth assumed a sardonic slant. 'Scored a point there, did I?' he mocked.

Unfortunately, he was all too correct, but that didn't stop her chin from lifting defiantly. 'As a matter of fact, it hasn't been decided yet.'

'And that doesn't tell you anything?' Fraser shook his head in disbelief.

Rowan shrugged the question away uneasily. Of course it raised suspicions, but she still needed work! 'Even if it did, why should you care?' she countered in despondent accents.

'God only knows, because you sure don't appear to!' His eyes raked over her savagely. 'Or maybe you're looking forward to the prospect of getting to know him more—er—intimately! Is that it?'

'No, that is not it!' she denied fiercely, and struggling to wrench free of his hold. 'Because I'm neither looking forward to, nor intending to get to know him any more *intimately*,' with corrosive emphasis, 'than I do now! So why don't you just leave me alone and concentrate on your own girl-friend! If it hadn't been for her, I wouldn't have to be considering Sean's offer at all!' She flung a bitter glance towards the house. 'Where is she, anyway? Inside, smirking over every word?'

Fraser retained his grip on her with infuriating ease. 'No, she's at home. It seems she developed a migraine when I told her I would appreciate it if she'd confine her attentions to her own staff in future,' he revealed wryly.

Astonishment had Rowan ceasing her futile attempts to escape. 'You argued over m-me?'

'I told you, I like to be in possession of all the facts when it relates to any termination of employment where my staff are concerned,' he reminded her in such an inflexible tone that she didn't wonder Erica had gone home in a huff. She didn't think for a minute that a headache had had anything to do with it. Neither was she the slightest bit sorry the other woman had received her come-uppance. It was no more than she deserved, in Rowan's mind. 'And if you're only considering Sean's offer because of what happened this afternoon,' Fraser continued, 'then I suggest you forget it.'

'I can't. I don't know if I'll get another,' she answered simply.

'Alice would welcome you back with open arms, you know.'

Was he implying she could go back to the plantation? A spark of hope flared inside her, and then just as quickly died. How ridiculous could she be? Of course he wasn't! He was merely playing cat and mouse. Biting at her lip, she averted her gaze to stare unseeingly at the ocean.

'I liked her too,' was all she said.

Fraser studied the flawless lines of the pensive profile thus presented to him with an unhurried diligence, then expelling a heavy breath, dragged a hand roughly through his hair. 'For someone who's so outwardly confident, you have a remarkably vulnerable look about you at times, honey,' he drawled in ironic tones.

Although the remark had Rowan swinging back to face him in dismay, it didn't really surprise her. For some strange, unknown reason, she *felt* extremely vulnerable whenever he was around. 'It's probably just a trick of the light,' she shrugged as nonchalantly as possible.

'Let's see, shall we?' he smiled lazily, and had pulled her from the shadows and into the revealing rays coming from the house before she could guess what he intended. It was only then that she realised he was now wearing shorts the same as she was, and likewise barefooted, his long powerfully muscled legs braced to keep his balance as she twisted violently away when he would have turned her face upwards. 'Well, are you going to work for Alice?' he caught her unawares by suddenly asking instead.

After having railed against being in his employ these last weeks, now all she unaccountably found she wanted to do was return to the plantation! Whatever was the matter with her? 'Are you . . . asking me to?' she queried tentatively, not wanting to take anything for granted.

'Since I forced you into resigning in the first place, don't you think I should?'

So it was only due to a guilty conscience that he was suggesting it, she mused wistfully, but didn't delve too deeply to discover why she should even have considered there might have been another reason. 'You don't have to, if you don't want to,' she averred in a whisper, giving him a way out if he wanted it.

'Rowan!' Now Fraser did turn her face up to his—exasperatedly. 'I'm asking you! All you have to do is answer, yes or no.'

She ran the tip of her tongue swiftly over her lips. 'Then yes . . . please.'

His responding gaze was so gentle that Rowan could hardly breathe. 'And that, I hope, proves I have not merely been waiting for a chance to dismiss you,' he said softly.

'I—I thought that was why you wanted me up at the house. To give you more opportunities to—to find fault,' she suddenly discovered herself being more candid than she had ever expected to be.

'Uh-uh!' He shook his head indolently as he lifted long strands of her hair from her shoulders and watched them slip between his fingers like a golden waterfall. 'That wasn't the idea at all.'

'Then what was?' she pushed out shakily. Fighting with Fraser had never affected her senses quite like this.

Still with her hair threaded between them, he smoothed the back of his fingers against her soft cheek. 'If Alice had to have an assistant, why not the most beautiful one?' he smiled crookedly.

Although the description had been applied to her many times before, Rowan still took it with a grain of salt. The more so where Fraser was concerned because it promptly reminded her of the time he'd said it once before, and not so very far distant.

'You're letting the moonlight influence you again,' she bantered in a more tremulous than amused tone.

'I never let the moonlight influence me,' he denied huskily, his thickly lashed eyes locking inescapably with hers. Then almost immediately he groaned, 'But— oh hell! Why did you have to come here tonight?' as he cupped her face between both hands and his lips came down on hers with a devastating insistence.

Currents of fire immediately coursed through Rowan, scattering her senses and her inhibitions, and provoking a response she was unable to control. Seemingly of their own volition her slender arms wound themselves about the firm column of his neck, her fingers exploring the broad width of his shoulders beneath the silk knit of his shirt, and her lips parting willingly beneath his as her curving form unconsciously pressed closer to the hard, stirring warmth of his.

Fraser's mouth sought the sensitive cord at the side of her arching throat, the tip of his tongue teasing it to throbbing heights, and then with a smothered exclamation he swept her into his arms and began carrying her effortlessly towards the house.

Caught as she was in a maelstrom of whirling emotions, there was no thought of demurring in Rowan's mind, only an ungovernable desire that he continue the exhilarating assault on her unbelievably aroused feelings, and with her arms still linked about his neck she laid her head unresistingly against his shoulder.

Passing through the sitting room, Fraser made for a bedroom at the front of the house, an unspoken question flickering in the depths of his darkly grey eyes as they connected with sultry, half closed brown ones and he lowered her gently on to the wide, blue-quilted bed. A question Rowan answered with a soft, indistinct moan as she pulled his head down to her eagerly waiting lips again.

Dear God, but she loved the way he made love, she thought shakily; the intoxicating way he kissed her, the fiery touch of his caressing fingers, but most of all came the sudden realisation, she loved *him*!

The unexpected revelation had her stiffening involuntarily for a second, the movement causing Fraser to raise his head quizzically, but with the beginnings of a shy smile playing about her lips she shook her head faintly and, allowing her emotions full rein, plucked at his shirt nervously.

'Take it off,' she whispered urgently, selfconsciously, and when he willingly complied ran trembling fingertips over the muscular, bronzed flesh now exposed.

'Rowan...!' He shuddered convulsively and claimed her lips again.

With her hands trapped between them she could feel his heart beating as heavily and unevenly as her own, and then hers was pounding even faster as he untied the halter strap of her top and pushed the brief scrap of material aside. In the dim light coming from the sitting room her honey-skinned breasts showed taut and full, the nipples enlarged and erect as they thrust upwards, inviting his attention, and a galvanising tremor lanced through her as he cupped one swelling mound in his hand and, lowering his head, guided the rosy peak towards his mouth.

Rowan gasped feverishly, the action intensifying the effect of his caressing lips and tongue, and as her clutching fingers tangled within his dark hair she moaned helplessly. Her flushed and heated body felt as if it would never be cool again, but incredibly it was burning even hotter a few moments later when Fraser's mouth proceeded to trace a scorching path downwards across her flat stomach, and after he had deftly unfastened her shorts, beyond.

'Oh, no! Please ... you can't ...!' she choked imploringly, and grabbed at his head in a frantic effort to prevent him going any further.

The abrupt ringing of the telephone diverted them both, although Fraser showed no inclination to answer it as he slid upwards to murmur confidently, thickly, against the hectic pulse at the base of her throat, 'It'll stop. No one actually knows I'm here.' He lifted his head and his gaze met hers ruefully. 'But some people's timing sure as hell leaves a lot to be desired!'

Rowan's long lashes fanned down protectively on to her stained cheeks. The interruption and its resulting subtle change in mood was only serving to remind her just how provocative and wanton her responses had been, and now waves of embarrassment were beginning to overtake her at the thought that he might guess how deeply her emotions were involved, or perhaps even worse, believe such behaviour was normal for her.

'M-maybe it's Evan,' she offered tremulously, laying a shielding arm across her breasts.

'I doubt it.' Fraser shook his head, and resolutely removing her arm, bent to kiss lingeringly each still throbbing nipple.

Rowan's whole body quivered at his touch. 'It could be important,' she only just managed to get out weakly.

'I don't know about important, but they're certainly bloody persistent!' he growled, and expelling a heavy breath, rolled off the bed and on to his feet in one lithe, catlike movement.

Momentarily, Rowan remained where she was, watching as he disappeared into the sitting room, and desperately attempting to regain control over her determinedly unruly feelings. But hearing the phone finally stop its penetrating ringing and Fraser begin to speak, she hastily gained her own feet and rapidly rearranged her dishevelled clothing. She was only too aware just what the outcome would be if she was still there when Fraser finished on the telephone, and although her heart might have welcomed his physical possession, her head judiciously counselled against it.

No matter how she felt about him, she could never expect him to reciprocate her feelings. Their worlds were too far apart for that, and besides, she had probably only been a handy substitute for Erica this evening, anyway. And one night's pleasure wasn't worth the pain all her ensuing mornings would bring, knowing she had allowed herself to be used as nothing more than a temporary diversion.

To her relief she heard Fraser speaking again, and slipping into the hall unnoticed, she tiptoed to the front door and let herself out on to the porch. From there, it was only a few steps before she was back on the beach again, but this time running as fast as she could in the direction of the Bay.

CHAPTER SEVEN

ROWAN didn't see Fraser again until breakfast the following morning, but fortunately by then she had both her thoughts and her feelings well marshalled, which enabled her to return his initial sardonic, brow-raising glance with at least some degree of equanimity. After breakfast, when she returned to the office to complete the cleaning she'd cursorily begun the preceding afternoon, and without Alice's and Evan's constraining presence, it was something of another matter, however.

Actually, she had chosen that particular time to do the office because most days Fraser spent the early mornings either out on the plantation or down at the factory, but to her discomfiture she discovered he had altered his routine that morning for some reason, and on entering the office she found him at his desk sorting through a sheaf of papers.

'I'm sorry, I didn't know you were here. I'll come back later,' she proposed immediately she realised her mistake.

'It doesn't matter, you won't disturb me,' he looked up to shrug. And a particular nuance in his voice had Rowan wondering whether he meant she, personally, wouldn't disturb him, or the work she intended doing. 'I'm only collecting some information I want to take north with me.'

'Take north with you?' The enquiry was out before she could stop it.

'Mmm, that's right.'

It could hardly have been called informative, and Rowan touched her teeth to her lower lip indecisively. 'W-will you be away long?' she asked in stilted accents.

Fraser continued with what he was doing. 'A few weeks, maybe.' Suddenly he cast her a highly mocking glance. 'Why, does it matter?'

He was meaning to her, of course, and she shook her head swiftly. 'No, n-naturally it doesn't,' she denied, albeit not very positively. As it happened, she wasn't sure whether she found the thought of his absence relieving or disappointing. 'I'll leave you to your collecting in peace, then,' taking a step towards the door.

'I said, it doesn't matter,' Fraser reminded her somewhat curtly, halting her. His expression became wry. 'Besides, I wanted a word with you, in any case.'

Rowan sucked in an apprehensive breath. 'What about?'

'Guess!' he taunted in a tone drenched with mockery.

'The—the job?' she stammered evasively.

He leant indolently back in his chair. 'Well, I guess that all depends on just which job you're referring to, doesn't it?' he drawled.

'Which job?' Rowan repeated perplexedly, and not a little warily.

'Mmm, this one, or . . .,' he paused, his eyes shading sardonically, 'the one you pulled on me last night.'

Although she flushed rather guiltily, Rowan refused to see it in the same light. 'I did nothing of the kind,' she denied on a rising note. 'I merely c-considered it an—an appropriate time to leave.'

'While my attention was conveniently engaged elsewhere!'

She shifted restlessly beneath his scornful gaze. 'You could have wanted privacy for your call,' she shrugged lamely.

'Not where Erica's concerned,' he divulged the identity of his caller slowly—deliberately, she suspected. 'She's never one to mind displaying her feelings, as you should know. Apparently she saw the house lights from the headland and surmised that that's where I was.'

'I see.' Rowan gazed down disconsolately at the carpet. So they'd patched up their differences, had they? She had been right in thinking she was only a substitute for the other woman. Even though she knew she could never expect it to be any different, the thought still had the power to hurt, unbearably, and it was only by calling on her pride that she managed to lift her head challengingly high. 'Well, at least that must have been some compensation for you. Your evening wasn't entirely a wash-out, was it?' she gibed.

Fraser's brows peaked expressively. 'You're suggesting I should be satisfied with a telephone call after having your shapely, naked, and so very sensuous self in my bed?' he quizzed drily as his eyes swept boldly up and down her body.

Rowan crimsoned with mortification. 'I wasn't naked!' she blurted. It was the only point she could think to dispute.

'It was only a matter of time, though, wasn't it?' His mouth shaped provokingly.

'You c-can't be certain of that,' she attempted to deny, weakly.

'Because you're a natural born tease who prefers to kiss and run?'

The unexpected charge had furrows of confusion

marring her wide forehead. 'I don't know what you mean.'

'No?' he mocked, rising to his feet and moving around the desk towards her. Rowan managed to stand her ground—just. 'Then how would you describe your habit of coming on so strong when you're kissed, and then promptly backing off at the first opportunity, hmm?' He tapped her emphasisingly under the chin with one long forefinger as he passed on his way to a filing cabinet at the other end of the room.

Rowan swivelled round, following his progress with pensive eyes. 'It's not a habit. I—I just don't think it's wise to become involved with one's employer, that's all,' she offered excusingly. There was no way she could explain that it was only he who had ever elicited such an unreserved response from her in the first place.

In the act of withdrawing a file from the top drawer of the cabinet, Fraser paused, a wry curve tilting his lips sideways as he turned his head in her direction. 'Except that, as I recall, on neither occasion were you actually in my employ,' he drawled.

'Last night I was!' she contended, even though it would probably have been more correct to say she'd been between periods of employment at the time.

As Fraser obviously considered her to have been, for he immediately countered, 'That's debatable!' Removing the file now, he inclined his head sardonically as he passed her again on his way back to the desk. 'And so's the question as to just how wise you would have been if Erica's call hadn't interrupted us.'

Another scarlet tide washed over Rowan's cheeks. She also doubted wisdom would have been uppermost in her mind under those circumstances. 'I—well, whatever, it's not something I really wish to discuss,' she faltered selfconsciously. 'Unless the matter holds some more profound meaning for you, of course,' she added, defensively pert.

'Uh-uh,' he replied so laconically, so unconcernedly, that Rowan felt a moment's despondency. Then suddenly he smiled, and just as rapidly her heart began to pound, as always. 'I don't believe in becoming involved with any of my staff,' he advised lazily, but pointedly for all that.

Why would he, when he had Erica, plus any number of glamorous others on hand? she grimaced tartly. The idea was dispiriting and almost peevishly she plugged in the vacuum cleaner and switched it on.

'Aren't you going to dust first?' Fraser's voice reached her above the noise of the machine.

'What? Oh, yes, I forgot.' She pulled a wry face as she turned the cleaner off again, and retrieving the duster from the back pocket of her jeans began wielding it diligently. Her previous thoughts remained with her, though, and presently prompted her into enquiring as casually as possible, 'Are you going on your own?'

'Where?'

'I don't know,' she shrugged somewhat irritatedly. 'You just said north.'

'Oh, there.' He shook his head negatively. 'No, I'll take someone with me, I expect.'

Rowan scowled in a disgruntled fashion at the wall in front of her and slammed the drawers of the filing cabinet closed with unnecessary force. 'And—er—when will you be leaving?'

'Tomorrow morning, most likely.'

She turned her attention to the bookshelf beside his desk. 'By car?'

'As far as Southleigh, yes.' Until then, Fraser had been answering without taking his eyes from the papers before him, but now he turned to look at her whimsically. 'You're positively burning with curiosity this morning, aren't you, honey?' he commented drily.

'Sorry,' she apologised with forced offhandedness, preparing to move behind his chair, but coming to a halt on finding him deliberately positioning himself to block her path. 'I didn't realise it was against the rules to show some interest.'

'It isn't,' he denied wryly, his ebony-lashed eyes unwavering as they watched her expressive face. 'Although one wonders just what caused such a change of attitude when, until now, you've shown a distinct preference for not speaking to me at all unless it was absolutely unavoidable. It wouldn't have something to do with the fact that I'm leaving, by any chance, would it?'

Rowan could feel her pulse thudding uncomfortably in her throat and swallowed convulsively. Thank God he thought that was the reason for her sudden interest! 'Quite possibly,' she was consequently more than willing to concede. 'After all, why shouldn't I return the compliment when you've made it so obvious right from the beginning that you're only waiting for the day when Tanya and I leave?'

'Then, if that was the case, why did I offer you your job back last night?'

'Because your conscience dictated you more or less had to, I suppose, otherwise I expect it would've been very different,' she retorted, seeking to continue hiding the real reason for her interest by attacking instead. 'Or maybe it was just because Sean . . .' She halted abruptly, an expression of dismay crossing her features. 'Sean! I was supposed to see him this morning to discuss the position he offered me!'

Impassively hunching a wide shoulder, Fraser returned his attention to his work. 'Then you'd better ring him and let him know it's not necessary now, hadn't you?' he suggested in faintly caustic tones.

Rowan was only too happy to do so. It would not only give her the opportunity to escape the office, which seemed both prudent and imperative at the moment, but would also enable her to question Alice regarding his apparently impending departure. A course she berated herself for not following originally, since that wouldn't have revealed, to him at least, her seemingly uncontrollable preoccupation with his movements.

'I'll do it now,' she took up the suggestion swiftly, and made to take her equipment with her.

'You can leave that. I'll be out of here shortly,' Fraser advised, his lips curving wryly, as if sensing her desire to avoid any further discussion on the subject, and with a small, discomfited nod of acknowledgement she left empty-handed.

Her ensuing phone call from the house didn't take long, but although Sean sounded a trifle disappointed to hear of the change in her plans, he still accepted her decision with such equanimity that it brought a rueful smile to Rowan's lips, and she wasn't quite certain whether she should have been pleased or piqued by his unperturbed reaction. A smile which was still in place when she left the study and met Alice walking, albeit somewhat awkwardly, down the hall.

'I take it that means you're glad to be back,' the housekeeper remarked on the lingering smile approvingly. Apart from showing her surprise, and then satisfaction, on seeing Rowan earlier, there had been little time for her to comment on her assistant's return so far.

'You could say that,' Rowan conceded, but without actually answering in the affirmative.

In truth, it was a question she could easily have answered either way, for having suddenly realised that she had idiotically allowed herself to become emotionally involved with her boss, she now found, confusingly, that both staying and leaving had points in their favour—and for exactly the same reason!—because she loved him.

By staying she would at least have some connection with Fraser, even though she doubted that would provide much comfort after a while if he was continually in Erica's company, but leaving ... well, that would be the final break and, Erica notwithstanding, right at the moment she doubted even more strongly if she could bring herself to take that irreversible step just yet.

'Well, I'm certainly glad to have you back,' Alice smiled fondly at her. 'And I pinned Fraser's ears back for him, I can tell you, when I heard the whole reason for your resignation ... which you omitted to mention.' She eyed the girl walking beside her sternly.

Rowan merely shrugged noncommittally in response to her last comment, but the thought of *anyone* taking Fraser to task, and especially on her account, appealed greatly to her sense of humour and she couldn't restrain the bubble of infectious laughter which rose inside her.

'I bet he wasn't too happy about that,' she grinned explicitly.

'Ruefully resigned, is how I'd put it, I think, since he'd only just discovered the truth of the matter for himself,' the housekeeper recalled, her lips twitching wryly.

'And now I understand he's—er—going away for a few weeks,' put in Rowan nonchalantly, trying to ease the conversation around to what she most wanted to discover. 'Do you know where to?'

'Is he?' Alice countered instead of replying, her greying brows peaking in obvious surprise. 'That's the first I've heard of it.' A slight frown and she went on. 'Although, on thinking about it, I suppose it's not really all that unexpected. I know he's been considering expanding the business for some time now.'

An unbelievable feeling of relief flooded through Rowan. 'Oh, so it's a business trip he's contemplating, then?' She couldn't be positive, of course, but if that was the case it was far less likely that Erica would be accompanying him, wasn't it?

'Well, I presume it is,' Alice frowned again, a little indecisively. 'It all depends where he's going, I guess.'

'I just heard north,' supplied Rowan in her most careless tone.

'Hmm . . .' The older woman's lips pursed thoughtfully. 'That's more than likely what it'll be then.'

'So who will be going with him? Evan?'

'I shouldn't think so. Why, are you concerned on your friend's behalf?' Alice's brown eyes twinkled.

'Oh, no, I was just wondering, that's all, because I understand he's not going on his own,' Rowan managed to shrug lightly. She hadn't been thinking of Tanya at all, actually. Taking a deep breath, she plunged on, 'It wouldn't be Erica, then, would it?'

'Erica Melville, you mean?' Alice's brows jumped skywards. 'Whatever makes you ask that?'

'I—well, I've noticed she seems very—er—possessive where Fraser's concerned.'

'Mmm, she's certainly that,' Alice laughed suddenly,

ironically. 'And if she did try to invite herself along, it wouldn't be for the first time, but I doubt she'd be any more successful than previously. Fraser's never been one to mix business with pleasure. No, I'd say it's most probably Dirk who'll be accompanying him,' mentioning the plantation's young manager.

Rowan could barely suppress a smile of satisfaction, then she speculated ruefully if she wasn't something of a masochist as she proposed with false, aching gaiety, 'Maybe Erica is going to be that wife you keep telling Fraser he should be considering.'

'I sincerely hope not!' The housekeeper's reply was immediate and straight to the point. 'There's been quite a number of others over the years who I'd rather see fill that position than that somewhat patronising young woman.' She sighed. 'Not that it's my choice to make, of course, or even to comment upon, I suppose, but I must admit he's been seeing more of her these last few weeks than he ever has done before.'

Feeling far less satisfied now—in fact, she felt distinctly dissatisfied—Rowan grimaced sourly. If she didn't like the answer, she had no one but herself to blame for having brought up the matter in the first place, she castigated inwardly. A slightly encouraging thought occurred. 'Although he didn't appear very taken with the idea when you mentioned the subject that first afternoon I came to work in the house, did he?' she recalled on a pleasurable note.

'N-o,' Alice granted slowly, meditatively, and fixing her assistant with a wryly subtle glance. 'But then I'm not quite sure just why you're so interested in whether he's contemplating marriage or not. It wouldn't have anything to do with the fact that you appeared extremely flushed when you came face to face with him in the breakfast room this morning, would it?'

Considering his appearance had promptly reminded her all too vividly of their last few moments together the night before, Rowan wouldn't have been surprised if she'd gone scarlet from head to toe! 'Did I? I can't imagine why,' she half choked, half laughed nervously. Alice was too observant, and too astute, for comfort. 'And as for—for the other ... well, you already know my feelings regarding both the Delaneys on that score.'

'Then it's a pity you haven't the courage of your convictions, isn't it?' put in Alice drily.

'I don't follow you,' Rowan frowned.

'Well, if Fraser is as—er—fickle, was the way you put it, I believe, in his dealings with the opposite sex as you accuse him of being, there's no call for you to be so worried about the thought of him marrying, is there?' The older woman smiled banteringly and, turning sharply, disappeared through the doorway into the kitchen.

'Alice!' Rowan hurried after her in dismay. 'That's r-ridiculous! I couldn't care less if Fraser married!' she denied for her own protection.

'Couldn't you?' Alice looked at her innocently, and then gave a little shrug. 'Oh, well, if you say so, love.'

Rowan sighed in a mixture of despair and exasperation. 'You don't believe me, do you?'

Alice didn't say, she just smiled, eloquently, and had Rowan's lips tilting wryly in response.

'Well, I don't!' she insisted. 'Why should I?'

'You really want me to answer that?' The housekeeper glanced at her askance.

'I don't see why not.' The words were indifferent even if the speaker wasn't.

However, instead of doing as almost challenged,

Alice chose to alter the subject entirely by enquiring, 'Have you ever considered taking a permanent job instead of doing casual work all the time, Rowan?'

Caught unawares, but both relieved and grateful for the change of topic, Rowan took a while to answer. 'There aren't many permanent positions available these days when you haven't been trained for anything in particular,' she disclosed at length.

'And like a lot of young people, you enjoy moving around, I suppose?'

'Not always. It's just that so far we've never found anywhere we really wanted to stay, and when you haven't a home of your own to return to, well . . .' hunching a slender shoulder impassively, 'you just tend to keep moving. And talking of moving, I think I'd better be, because I still haven't finished those offices yet,' Rowan relayed hastily, wanting to make good her departure before Alice could perhaps return to less comfortable subjects. It had proved almost as nerve-racking questioning her as it had Fraser about his proposed trip.

'Oh, but . . .' the housekeeper began.

'I'll be back in about an hour,' Rowan broke in determinedly, and had pushed out through the flyscreen door before the older woman had a chance to protest further.

On finding the main office unoccupied at last, Rowan set about cleaning the room as quickly and as efficiently as she could before her employer returned, and then turned her attention to the remainder of the building. The last area to receive her ministrations was around the reception desk, and immediately she came into view Hazel, who was now present, beckoned her over and with a smile on her lips, Rowan moved across to her quickly.

'I wanted to thank you for explaining to Fraser what happened yesterday afternoon,' she said appreciatively.

'Oh, think nothing of it,' Hazel grinned, dismissing her gratitude lightly. 'I was only too pleased to be able to help. It didn't seem fair that you should lose your job just because Erica was in a bitchy mood, because I know from personal experience what she can be like. Why, before I was married, she even accused *me* of chasing after the boss!' She gave her head an incredulous shake, her expression becoming thoughtful as she went on to query interestedly, 'But—er—while we're on such delicate subjects, what's this I hear about Tanya and Evan?'

The rapid change of topic had Rowan staring at her blankly. 'I don't know,' she shrugged. 'What have you heard?'

'That matters aren't too cordial between them at the moment.'

'Oh?' The arch of Rowan's winged brows became even more prominent. 'They seemed okay last night.' Admittedly, it had been an almost silent journey home from the Bay, but she'd merely put that down to tiredness due to the late hour. 'Who told you otherwise?'

'Coral Raymond,' the other girl divulged obligingly. 'Apparently Tanya mentioned something about it to her this morning.'

'Something about what?' she asked anxiously.

Hazel's expression became lugubrious. 'I was hoping you'd be able to tell me that,' she confessed wryly.

'Sorry.' Rowan's mouth assumed a rueful shape. Hazel's penchant for wanting to know everything that happened on the plantation was notorious. 'But you appear to know more than I do already.' A slight frown began to crease her forehead. 'So exactly what did Tanya tell Coral?'

'More or less, only that she wasn't particularly happy with Evan at present.'

'That's all?'

'As I said,' Hazel grimaced, 'I was hoping you'd be able to fill in the details.'

'Oh, well, I expect it's only something minor and it will all be forgotten by tomorrow,' predicted Rowan lightly, doing her best to ignore the insidious sense of foreboding that was creeping over her. Of one thing she was certain, though. Despite her dismissive forecast, she would be ensuring that she saw her friend when she left work that afternoon in order to discover just how matters did stand between Tanya and her latest love.

'You're probably right,' allowed Hazel with a sigh, then grinned, 'I was just looking forward to a nice little bit of intrigue to keep me occupied while the boss is away looking for land, that's all.'

Temporarily diverted, Rowan eyed her speculatively. So that was why he was going, was it? 'He's planning to start another plantation, is he?' she probed.

'Mmm, although not for himself, of course. This one's quite large enough,' Hazel laughed.

'Then who?' Rowan frowned.

'A syndicate that wants him to set up and oversee a plantation for them. Delaneys don't just grow and process their own produce, you know. They also supply other plantations with their plants—the reason we have such a large grafting section—as well as providing a consulting service. And since negotiations were finalised with this particular group a week or so ago . . .' Hazel spread her hands significantly wide.

'I didn't realise.' Rowan shook her head in amazement. She had guessed, just from his manner, that Fraser was extremely capable in his own field, but until now she'd had no conception just how knowledgeable he was about it too. 'Does he often develop new plantations for others?'

'No, this is actually the first he's agreed to start from scratch, although he does oversee a few places around the district, but he's been considering expanding the consulting side of the business for a while, and he figures it'll probably be less of a hassle if he has control right from the beginning instead of being called in to solve the problems which always seem to arise once the project's under way.'

'As well as being extremely lucrative,' deduced Rowan drily.

'Yes, well, it's certainly that,' Hazel conceded. 'But why shouldn't it be when he's accepting such a responsibility?'

'No reason, I guess,' Rowan shrugged. Except that it only served to emphasise more strongly the unbridgeable disparity between Fraser's background and her own, she sighed mutely. And with that dispiriting thought she returned to the work at hand.

The remainder of the day seemed to stretch endlessly for Rowan as she awaited her chance to speak to Tanya, but eventually the afternoon began drawing to a close and when her friend walked out through the side door of the factory she was already waiting for her.

'Rowan! You must be psychic!' Tanya exclaimed as she saw her. 'I was just intending to walk up to the house in order to see you.'

'Oh? What about?' sounded Rowan cautiously as of

one accord they began retracing her steps up the hill.

'Nothing in particular. Just a chat,' Tanya maintained with a shrug. Her head tilted quizzically to one side. 'What brought you down here?'

'The desire for a chat,' copied Rowan in dry tones, and looking at each other they both laughed, ruefully. They were too well acquainted not to see through each other's feigned nonchalance.

'You've heard about Evan's and my squabble last night, I gather?' Tanya surmised.

Rowan nodded, admitting whimsically, 'Something of the sort did reach my ears, although I've no idea what it was actually about.'

'Oh, it was all a storm in a teacup really,' her friend decried airily. 'Just because I had three dances with that hunk of a mate of his from Southleigh, Glynn Terrill, there was no need for him to make such a production out of it, or to spend the rest of the evening ogling that neighbour of his, Claudette, in retaliation.' She made a dismissing gesture with one hand and smiled. 'Anyway, it's all over now. We made up this morning.'

Unfortunately, Rowan couldn't match her insouciance, because her previous sense of foreboding was suddenly back in full force. 'But why would you want to dance that number of times with his friend?' she ventured tentatively. 'I thought you were supposed to be in love with Evan.'

'Well, yes—I am, of course,' asserted Tanya, although somewhat flusteredly, which did nothing to alleviate her companion's mounting feeling of *déjà vu*. 'But that doesn't make me unappreciative of every other male I meet,' and—and Glynn really is something.' She smiled persuasively. Or was it reminiscently? wondered Rowan with restive apprehension. 'You'd know what I mean if you met him.'

'Hmm . . . I'll take your word for it.' There didn't seem much else she could say.

'Besides, even if—even if Evan and I did part company, it wouldn't make any difference to you, would it?' Tanya hurried on, awkwardly offhanded. 'I mean, I know you never wanted to work for Fraser in the first place, and especially not in the house, so you'd have no—er—objection to moving on if things didn't work out, would you?'

Rowan's stomach contracted. So that *was* the way the wind was blowing, after all! 'No, I wouldn't mind in the slightest,' she alleged on a valiantly uncaring note in an effort to convince herself as much as her friend. Since she had no intention of telling Tanya just how she felt about their employer, it would probably be for the best if she did allow that girl to unwittingly make the decision to leave for her. She already knew nothing but heartbreak could come from her staying, and as well as that, if she did remain for any length of time there was always the chance she might unconsciously reveal the true state of her feelings to Fraser. And it was that humiliating thought, more than any other, which had her repeating resolutely, 'Not in the slightest!'

'I didn't think you would,' Tanya beamed gaily, and obviously relieved. 'Not that I'm saying I'm considering a move at the moment, of course, because I'm not. But it's as well to be prepared for any eventuality, don't you think?'

'That's the way we've always played it,' Rowan shrugged. But although Tanya might have deluded herself into believing she wasn't considering a move, Rowan wryly suspected she knew better. She had seen

her friend fall in and out of love too many times in the
past not to recognise the initial signs of her cooling
interest now.

They walked on in companionable silence for a few
minutes, each occupied with her own thoughts, then
Tanya glanced at the girl beside her enquiringly.

'You know, you never did get around to explaining
last night how come you agreed to return to work at
the plantation. I would have thought that after all
that's happened, nothing short of wild horses would
have been able to drag you back here,' she mused.

'So did I . . . once,' Rowan half laughed a trifle self-
mockingly. 'But, as usual, the prospects for work at
the Bay didn't exactly set one alight,' provided one
didn't include Sean's offer which no doubt could have
proved scorching, she added privately, 'so when
Fraser asked me to return . . .'

'He *asked* you?' Tanya interrupted, her tone openly
incredulous.

'Only because of an undoubtedly rare attack of
guilty conscience,' Rowan relayed sardonically. 'He
probably felt he had to after Hazel had explained that
it wasn't altogether my fault, as well as saving him
the trouble of finding a replacement assistant for
Alice.'

'Oh, well, at least you've got work again, and
somewhere nice to stay.' Tanya's eyes rose admiringly
to the house on the hill before them. 'It's certainly a
home and a half, isn't it? I wonder if we'll ever own
anything even a quarter as nice.'

Rowan's gaze followed her companion's wistfully.
'Only if we rob a bank,' she part laughed, part
grimaced. 'Or . . .' she hesitated, 'you marry Evan.'

Momentarily, Tanya looked a little discomfited.
'Mmm, but then it's not really Evan's house, is it? It's

Fraser's,' she classified finally on a seemingly allayed breath.

Rowan merely nodded, ironically. If she'd wanted any further proof that her friend's interest in Evan was beginning to fade, then that sudden show of uneasiness on Tanya's part had just provided it.

CHAPTER EIGHT

THE following morning Rowan saw Fraser only briefly before he left—in company with Dirk Lindley, the plantation manager, as Alice had presupposed—and then only because the housekeeper insisted she accompany her to the porch in order to see the two men off. But while Alice fussily supervised Dirk's loading of the luggage into the car, Fraser turned and unexpectedly tilted Rowan's rather sombre face up to his.

'I imagined you to be all smiles at this point,' he drawled tauntingly.

Rowan swallowed hard, but refused to drop her gaze in case the action inadvertently revealed just how effortlessly he disconcerted her. 'And when you've finally departed, I probably shall be,' she lied, defensively brash.

Sable lashes lowered to give his face a threatening cast, but his smoke-coloured eyes remained mocking. 'And to think that only the night before last you were willingly sharing my bed!' he tut-tutted.

It was impossible for Rowan to hide her discomposure now, as she guessed he knew it would be, and she looked away embarrassedly. 'Do you have to keep referring to that?' she snapped.

'Why not?' A lazy smile pulled his lips sideways. 'It happened.' A purposeful hand ensured her gaze returned to his again. 'Whether you like to admit it or not.'

'So, who does like to admit their mistakes?' she quipped audaciously.

'Was it?'

Oh, God! He hadn't guessed the reason for her lack of resistance, had he? 'Of—of course it was!' Rowan spluttered on a desperate note. 'Wh-why, you even said yourself you don't like becoming involved with any of your staff! And it's not as if—as if it's likely to happen again. I mean, you have Erica again now to fulfil any needs you might have in that regard, don't you?' Her brown eyes shone with an unknowingly bitter light. 'In any event, I may not even still be here when you return,' she disclosed unintentionally in the heat of the moment.

'Oh, and why not?' Fraser's eyes narrowed intently, all trace of his previous tolerance disappearing.

She moved uncomfortably from one foot to the other, cursing her runaway tongue. 'I—why—well, it's quite possible. I don't know exactly how long you're planning to be gone, do I?' she countered evasively.

'*Why*, Rowan?' he ignored her excuse in order to press determinedly.

Pearly white teeth caught at a soft underlip. 'I think matters may be cooling off somewhat between Tanya and Evan,' she confessed in a grudging, chagrined tone.

'I could have told you that,' Fraser grinned suddenly—mockingly, she thought—although that still didn't stop a wild sensation from racing along her spine in response to the beguiling shaping of his sensuous mouth.

'Meaning, I told you so, I suppose!' she charged, and not a little resentfully.

'Could be,' he wasn't averse to conceding in a lazily goading drawl. He lowered his head to within disturbing centimetres of hers. 'And now I'll tell you a couple more things too, honey. One, I don't give a damn what happens between those two while I'm away, but *you* had better be here when I return. And two, if I hear you've gone back to hitching rides during my absence, you won't be able to sit for a week by the time I've finished with you.'

'You wouldn't dare!' Rowan blazed immediately, and then gulped as she saw the steely, inflexible look in his eyes. Oh yes, he would! She reluctantly, but prudently, decided to concentrate on his first imperious dictate. 'And just what makes it so essential that *I* be here when you return? Don't tell me you're beginning to find me indispensable!' Her eyes widened sarcastically.

'No worries, I won't,' he returned, equally satirical. 'But for some unaccountable reason Alice apparently does, so for her sake at least it's surely not expecting too much for you to stick around while she's incapacitated, because Evan is going to have quite enough on his plate dealing with all aspects of the business—plus your flighty little friend, of course—without all the hassle of trying to find a replacement for you as well.'

'All right, I'll stay ... for Alice's sake!' Rowan abruptly found herself promising on a flaring note. He'd made her feel guilty by even contemplating leaving the housekeeper without help again. 'But just what do you mean, my *flighty* friend?'

'Well, isn't she?' He arched one brow expressively high.

'No!' she defended loyally. 'She's placid and softhearted, and thoughtful, and—and . . .'

'Capricious,' he put in drily. 'The same as Evan.'

A rueful smile began edging its way across her mobile lips. 'Well, maybe a little changeable at times,' she owned, then rallied almost immediately to gibe, 'Although look who's talking!'

The corners of Fraser's mouth took a decidedly goading upturn. 'Except that I've never yet led any female to believe I intended anything permanent to come of any relationship we might have together.'

No, he certainly didn't do that, Rowan recalled desolately, and was thankful when a hail from Dirk advised that the car was loaded. Perhaps, once Fraser was gone, she would be able to put both him, and such anguished thoughts, out of her mind for a while.

The only trouble was that as the ensuing days stretched into weeks, living in Fraser's home made it well nigh impossible for her to eject his memory from her thoughts at all, let alone for any length of time. So as Alice's leg recuperated, and Tanya's romance visibly deteriorated, Rowan went listlessly about her tasks, sensing what the inevitable outcome would be. As soon as the housekeeper had recovered, Tanya and herself would be leaving.

However, although her conscious recognised that as the most desirable course to follow—if only for her peace of mind—the less governable depths of her brain weren't nearly so co-operative as they constantly reminded her that it would mean never seeing Fraser again, and she spent many a wakeful night as the two opposing lines of thought battled against each other inside her head. The days soon proved to be even worse, though, for once the doctor pronounced Alice fit again and the cast was removed, there was considerably less for Rowan to do, so while her friend vacillated between staying a little longer or making the final break with Evan, she took to filling in more and more of her time at the plantation's nursery section in order to optimistically keep her mind occupied with less troublesome thoughts.

She liked working outdoors, and it was not only interesting but extremely satisfying as well to see the young plants growing strong and healthy, and knowing she'd had a hand in keeping them that way, even if it did mean getting somewhat scratched in the process by the harshly serrated leaves. It was also gratifying to discover her knowledge of the industry was growing too, for she was only just beginning to realise how many different strains of macadamia had now been produced, and just how the public's fickle eating tastes could present the grower with some headaches at times. One year Strain 333 might be all the rage, and then just as quickly go out of fashion, while 334 or 660 took its place, and when a tree needed fifteen years to reach full maturity, that did pose problems, notwithstanding that they could be re-grafted to change the variety up until they were about five years old.

Fraser had been gone for almost a month when Tanya finally came to the conclusion that Evan wasn't her Mr Right, after all, and understandably feeling rather less comfortable in his employ now, gave a week's notice of her intention to leave. Rowan, half regretfully, half relievedly, did the same, but at least now that Alice was fully recovered she didn't feel guilty in doing so. Distressed a little, she might have been, as was the older woman when she heard of her decision, but not guilt-ridden, because as far as she was concerned she had fulfilled her promise to stay for the housekeeper's sake. Which had been the only reason for Fraser insisting she remain, she reflected morosely.

No week had ever seemed so long to Rowan, and yet, conversely, so short either, and she sometimes found herself wondering whether Fraser knew or even cared now that Alice was better, that she was leaving shortly, for although she was aware he had regularly been in touch with Evan, she had no idea just what information passed between them.

Nevertheless, by the time her last day on the plantation arrived, she was still subconsciously, futilely, half hoping to hear something from her employer—just what, she couldn't have said, unless it was 'good riddance'—but as usual not so much as a word filtered back to her, and all that remained was for her to make her departure with as much poised, but feigned, unconcern as she could muster.

Unable to sit passively after dinner that evening, Rowan excused herself to Alice—Evan had gone visiting the neighbourly Claudette—and headed outside for a walk. She felt too restless, too disturbed, and just plain depressed, she supposed gloomily, to make polite, inconsequential conversation, and knowing it would be her last opportunity to wander among the peacefully rustling trees, as she often did in the evenings, she wanted to make the most of it.

Overhead the sky was inky black, but cloudless, the myriad stars shining with crystal clarity around the golden disc of a new moon which was bathing the earth below in a soft, mellow light. Passing through the gardens, Rowan slowly made her way between the neatly spaced rows of the plantation, her eyes misting involuntarily as they took in the tranquil scene laid before her, realising she would never see this place or its vibrant owner again. For the first time in her life she had found somewhere she could willingly have stayed for ever, only to have circumstances decree otherwise. Abruptly, the mist became an increasing blur as long-denied tears welled to the surface unbidden, and sinking down on to the ground with her back against one of the trees, she covered her face with her hands and cried as heartbrokenly as she had done at the orphanage on that sorrowful day so long ago.

How long her spate of weeping lasted, Rowan didn't know, but when at last it began to subside the grass around her was damp with dew, and rising wearily to her feet she brushed off her long cotton skirt mechanically as she decided against continuing her walk. At the moment all she felt like doing was seeking the mind-blanking deliverance of sleep. And so, with downbent head and dragging steps, she started back towards the house, but as she reached the garden a sound, or perhaps it was just something she sensed, caused her to look up, and she couldn't quell the audible gasp that escaped her to see Fraser's unmistakeable and commanding figure striding towards the verandah steps.

With disbelieving eyes, Rowan stood for a second as if turned to stone, her thoughts anything but still as they whirled in confusion. Why was he here, and why tonight of all nights? Had he completed his work, or had he just returned to check on the plantation in person? Had anyone known he intended coming, and if so, why hadn't it been mentioned? Then, with a despairing shake of her head, she seemed to regain the use of her limbs and, about-facing, fled for the concealing shadows of an arching poinciana. Having just been grieving over the fact that she would never see him again, she now felt compelled to avoid him at all costs.

Fast moving footsteps behind her advised that she hadn't been successful, though, and as she ducked beneath the first spreading branch she dashed her fingertips across still wet cheeks and spun to face him defiantly.

Fraser slowed but didn't stop, thereby forcing her to retreat before him. 'And just where were you running to?' he queried tautly.

'N-nowhere in particular,' she replied shakily, but continuing to angle her head challengingly high. 'I felt like some exercise, that's all.'

'Immediately you saw me, of course!'

Taking another step backwards, she found herself trapped against the trunk of the tree, making her eyes widen in dismay. 'Wh-why not? As I said, I felt like it.'

His hand shot out to ensnare her chin and force her face up to the light visible between the feathery leaves above. 'In the hopes that it would dry those tears?' he proposed sardonically.

'What tears?' she countered promptly, even as she lowered her eyelids protectively.

He ran the tip of a forefinger gently across her spikily closed lashes, and not surprisingly it came away wet. 'Those tears,' he reiterated softly.

Rowan's eyes flew open again in a panic at the thought of him guessing the reason for their dampness. 'Well, what about them?' she opted fretfully for attack now instead of denial. 'Crying isn't against the law, is it? I mean, not even you with all your orders and restrictions could expect . . .'

'What?' he cut in swiftly. 'You to keep your promise that you'd be here when I returned?'

'I didn't promise that! You d-didn't ask me t-to.' Her voice started to wobble ignominiously and it required a considerable effort to strengthen it again. 'I only promised to stay as long as Alice needed me.'

'And that's important to you, isn't it?'

'What is?'

'To be needed.'

'Don't be ridiculous!' she blustered frantically. 'I don't need anyone, and I don't want anyone to need me either! I never have!'

'Not even your own mother?' he probed quietly.

In the shocked silence that followed, Rowan could hear her breath rasping unevenly. 'What would you know about her?' she choked.

A muscle jumped at the side of his jaw. 'I know about her dumping you in an orphanage . . .'

'Who told you that?' she burst in on a raw note.

'Alice.'

'Alice!' she repeated in disbelief. 'Oh, how could she? She should have known I was only telling her in confidence.' Her eyes darkened bitterly. 'Or didn't she care?'

'Yes, she cared!' Fraser retorted. 'She cares about you very much, in fact . . . as you should damn well know!' He exhaled heavily. 'That's why I had to practically drag the information out of her.'

'Why should you bother?' she sniped bitterly.

'Because I was determined to discover just what caused those tragically insecure expressions one unexpectedly catches on your face at times.'

Rowan stiffened compulsively. 'Tragically insecure! *Me?*' she mocked, although none too steadily. 'You've got the wrong person, haven't you? I'm the brash, outspoken one. Ask anyone, they'll tell you the same.'

'Yeah, sure,' he drawled no less tauntingly. 'And that's why you were crying, is it? Because you're so secure and self-assured and confident?'

'That has nothing to do with it!' she flared defensively. 'And—and stop trying to push me into a corner! Haven't you something more constructive to do . . . like planting another tree, or something?'

Fraser's firm lips sloped wryly. 'Now that you mention it, yes, I have,' he acceded, and before she could ascertain his intention, had taken possession of her mouth in a hard and hungry kiss.

Despairing of the way her pulse immediately began to race, Rowan fought fiercely to break free, her hands beating blindly against his chest and then entwining within his dark hair and pulling at it sharply. No matter if she did love him, or that it was the last time she would probably ever be this close to him again, she wasn't going to be a convenient substitute for Erica again . . . *she wasn't*! With a muffled exclamation, Fraser pulled her arms down swiftly and pinioned them behind her back, his rugged form pressing her close against the tree, and his mouth continuing its persistent and unsparing exploration of hers.

'You're an arrogant, overbearing swine, Fraser Delaney, and I hate you!' she blazed when at last he condescended to release her unconsciously parted lips.

'And you're not a very accomplished liar, Rowan Adams,' he drawled in deeper tones than normal. 'So how about we try again, mm?' And he once more caught her unawares as he lowered his head to hers while she was still panicking over the significance of his words.

But now he wasn't giving her a chance to analyse them, because this time his lips weren't hard and dominant, they were sensuously persuasive, and she needed all her concentration to avoid surrendering, unreservedly, to their tantalising caress. There was an ache in her chest that threatened to suffocate her, and when Fraser's arms slid upwards along her arms to cradle her head between them she could feel her resistance beginning to crumble, and her own hands clenched stiffly at her sides in an effort to retain at least some control over her unruly emotions.

'For God's sake, stop fighting me, Rowan!' he groaned throatily against her quivering lips. 'I love you!'

Rowan shook her head disbelievingly, and drawing back, whirled out of his arms, her eyes filling with hot salty tears. 'You don't love me! You just want to *make* love to me!' she charged anguishedly.

'I won't deny that,' Fraser owned huskily behind her, and gathering her back against him, parted her hair in order to press his mouth to the sensitive nape of her neck, sending shivers of arousal speeding down her spine. 'But if I thought you'd stand still long enough to listen, I'd ask you to marry me.' His lips sought her neck again, his arms tightening about her convulsively. 'Because I do love you, honey. Oh, God, do I!'

Rowan tensed, and then easing out of his arms, turned to face him incredulously. 'You couldn't love me ... want to marry me,' she whispered, still not daring to believe.

Fraser's gaze held hers gently. 'Why couldn't I? Because you figure that if your own mother didn't love you enough to keep you, then no one else could either?'

She hunched a slim shoulder diffidently. 'It seemed r-reasonable to assume ...' Stopping, she pressed her lips together firmly. 'Besides, our backgrounds are too different. You should be saying all this to someone like Erica. She's got far more to offer than I have.'

'The hell she has!' He obviously wasn't of the same mind. 'And in any case,' he half smiled ruefully, 'I don't happen to care what Erica has to offer. My only interest revolves around a certain disconcerting little blonde.' His hands reached for her shoulders, his voice thickening resonantly. 'Because I suspect she has something far more precious than mere worldly goods to give me. And I'm right, aren't I, Rowan?'

She trembled uncontrollably. 'If you mean . . .'

'You know what I mean!' he broke in with a despairing groan, his arms enclosing her possessively. 'Or are you going to make me marry you before you'll finally admit it?'

'Would you?' Brown eyes sought grey wonderingly.

'Yes!' His reply was unequivocal. And so was the adoration she could see in his expression.

'Oh, Fraser!' Her voice quavered helplessly. 'You know I love you! I think I have ever since that night you first kissed me.' She buried her head shyly against his chest. 'Only I thought it was the gin making me feel the way I did.'

For a moment she could feel him shake with silent laughter, and her own lips began to curve in response. 'Then now do you think you could kiss me?' he turned her face up to his to ask.

Rowan didn't bother to reply aloud. She just slipped her arms around his neck and tugged his head down to willing lips, and let their uninhibited actions speak for her. The fervency of her kiss seemed to catch Fraser unprepared, but not for long, and then he was equalling it as his arms tightened like steel bands about her, enclosing them in a world of their own, and arousing within each of them burning desires only the other could satisfy.

'Dear lord, I want you so much I don't think I'll be able to stand the strain of waiting until we're married!' he murmured unsteadily quite some time later as he swept her high against his broad chest and carried her easily to a padded garden seat on the other side of the tree, where he sank down with her still cradled in his arms.

Rowan touched her fingers to his lips tenderly. 'You don't have to, if you don't want to,' she said simply, understanding how he felt. It was exactly the same for her too.

'That's what you said about me re-hiring you,' Fraser recalled with a lazily crooked smile that had her stomach turning somersaults. 'And my feelings are the same now as they were then. I want to.' That beguiling smile made another appearance. 'Besides, Alice would never forgive me if she ever discovered I'd—er—anticipated our married state, is how she would describe it, I believe. It was bad enough when you resigned, because didn't I get hauled over the coals for my part in that!'

Rowan's eyes twinkled disarmingly. 'Would anyone ever dare do such a thing?'

'Apart from you, you mean?' he retorted drily.

'Oh!' She looked at him mock-indignantly. 'When did I ever get a chance to put you in your place? You were always too busy putting me in mine!'

'Unsuccessfully, it seemed, on most occasions!' He shook his head in rueful remembrance.

'It didn't to me.' Her mouth tilted wryly. 'I thought you were the most arrogant man I'd ever met. And what's more,' she twisted around in order to give him the full benefit of her glowering expression, 'you were an absolute heel to me that first night at the beach house. You treated me like a tramp!'

Fraser grinned and pressed a kiss to the corner of her mouth. 'Initially, I thought you probably were,' he drawled impenitently. 'During those previous clashes I'd had with your group on the beach, you hadn't exactly been shy and retiring, my love . . . and I might add, nor were you when I kissed you.'

'But that was because of the gin!' she protested, and then gave a sheepish chuckle. 'At least, I thought it was at the time.'

'Don't worry, you weren't the only one that evening backfired on,' he laughed. 'Why else do you think I relented and allowed Evan to hire you both the next day?'

Rowan shook her head vaguely. 'I never could work that out.'

'Because after brusquely dismissing you—I'd suddenly realised I was beginning to find you too damned attractive for my own good—I then spent a very sleepless night thinking about a particularly tantalising little spitfire, and subconsciously wishing she was there beside me.' He traced the contours of her curving lips with a gentle forefinger, his eyes filling with whimsical laughter. 'I knew I should never have kissed you.'

'Do you regret it?' She sent him a highly provoking glance from under long, silky lashes.

'Does it look like it?' he growled, capturing her mouth with his and proceeding to convince her extremely satisfyingly.

'There was something else I could never understand either,' Rowan mused when he eventually released her and she had recovered her voice again. She lifted her eyes to his enquiringly. 'Why were you so against Evan becoming involved with Tanya? Originally, I thought it was because you didn't consider her good enough for him, but,' a frown descended on to her forehead, 'now I'm inclined to think it wasn't that at all . . . was it?'

Fraser didn't immediately say, but asked first, 'What made you change your mind?'

'Well, I began to suspect that may not have been the reason a while ago, but mainly, the fact that you want to marry me, I suppose,' she explained with a deprecating half laugh. 'I mean, if social standing was your criterion, you wouldn't be doing that, would you?'

'Thank you for that, at least.' He inclined his head wryly. 'Although if I ever hear you refer to yourself in such a deprecating manner again, there'll be trouble, believe me!' He cupped her face tenderly between his palms. 'No matter what you may have been led, or come, to believe over the years, I can assure you you're not a nobody, my love. You're something very special, and don't you ever forget it!'

Rowan smiled up at him somewhat mistily. 'You certainly know how to boost a girl's morale, don't you?' she quipped shakily.

'I figure it's about time someone did,' he smiled back. 'And especially when it's no more than the truth.' He paused. 'But to return to your question concerning Evan and Tanya . . . I admit that at first I suspected she might have only been out for what she could get, but after a while, and as much as it may surprise you, it was actually on Tanya's behalf that I was never in favour of their liaison. Knowing Evan's habit of playing fast and loose made me only too aware that it was more than likely nothing would come of the affair, and she could have been hurt in the process. Of course, the only thing wrong with that was, no one was particularly forthcoming with the information that she was as undependable as he was. Were they?' He eyed her mock-direfully.

'I—er—thought it wisest not to,' she dimpled irrepressibly. 'After all, I suppose they'll each find the right partner one day.' Pausing, she pressed her lips together worriedly. 'I'll feel badly springing our news on Tanya so suddenly, though. She's expecting us to leave in the morning.'

'Perhaps she'll prefer to remain in the district once she discovers you're staying,' Fraser suggested.

'She might, if there was more work available.'

'Then we'll just have to see that there is, won't we? And probably in Southleigh, for preference,' he added drily.

'Oh?' Rowan's forehead creased perplexedly. 'Why there, in particular?'

'You mean she hasn't told you about Glynn Terrill yet?' he countered with one dark brow arching meaningfully. 'Or has he already gone the same way as Evan?'

'No!' She tried to look reproving but ended by laughing. 'Not even Tanya falls out of love *that* quickly. But how did you know about Glynn?'

'I was at the dinner-dance when she met him, remember? And the signs were fairly obvious even then.'

'I see,' she smiled ruefully.

Fraser threaded his fingers meditatively between the long strands of her golden hair. 'But we have our own memories of that night, don't we, honey?'

'That was when I first realised I loved you,' she admitted shyly.

'And the night I discovered that if I couldn't make love to you, I didn't have the slightest desire to make love to anyone else,' he disclosed in roughened tones.

Rowan wound her arms about him tightly. 'I thought you were just using me as a substitute for Erica,' she whispered abjectly. 'And—and at first I thought that's what you were doing tonight too.'

'Oh, God, no!' Fraser denied vehemently. 'If

anything, she's probably been a bulwark against you!'

'*Against* me? But why?'

An oblique curve moulded his lips engagingly. 'Because, my delightful, adorable little darling, my life was proceeding very nicely, thank you, until you came along and systematically annihilated all my preconceived notions of a continuing, enjoyable bachelorhood!'

'Oh!' she gurgled not the least bit sympathetically. And as a sudden suspicion occurred, 'That wouldn't also be why you decided to go north as abruptly as you did, would it?'

'It would,' he owned, drily laconic. 'After you'd run out on me the night before, I figured I'd be doing myself a favour if I put some distance between us. You know, out of sight, out of mind?' Even white teeth showed in a self-mocking grin. 'Well, take my word for it, it doesn't work! Before we even reached the airfield in Southleigh I was wishing I hadn't left, and I've done nothing but think of you ever since. You steal into a man's blood like a fever, my love, but . . .' his eyes darkened ardently, 'I wouldn't have it any other way.'

'You really do say the nicest things,' she breathed adoringly, and rewarded him in the most pleasing way she knew how.

'And if you keep this up, you tempting little witch,' he murmured huskily against her lips as they nibbled sensuously at his, 'I know where we're going to end up!'

'Your bed, or mine?' she quizzed impishly.

'The way I'm feeling, I doubt we'd reach either!' Fraser retorted gruffly, and deliberately set her away from him.

Rowan nestled against him contentedly, revelling in

her new-found sense of security. 'Why did you come back tonight, Fraser?' she asked. 'Were you due to?'

'Only when I heard you were planning to leave,' he advised deeply. 'I knew I couldn't let you go without trying to stop you, but I left it as late as I dared in the hope that maybe that spark of emotion which always seemed to flare between us would have blazed into something stronger for you too during my absence.'

'Instead, it already had,' she smiled up at him dreamily. 'I wonder what Alice will say when she finds out.'

'Somehow, I suspect she already knows,' he drawled lazily. 'But we can go and see, if you like.'

'Not just yet,' she demurred softly, pressing closer to his muscular frame, and with her lips parting spontaneously to receive his already descending mouth. 'I don't feel like sharing you with anyone right at the moment.'

A sentiment with which Fraser obviously concurred, because as it so happened, quite some considerable time was to elapse before they eventually got around to seeing Alice.

Harlequin® Plus

A WORD ABOUT THE AUTHOR

As a child Kerry Allyne often occupied herself by spinning short stories, without ever actually imagining she might write anything for publication. But when her youngest child started school, Kerry took out her trusty typewriter and set about trying to fill in the days by writing a novel.

For inspiration she had only to look out her window over a garden filled with flowering frangipani, hibiscus and azalea. For a title she had only to think about Australia's wet season (summer), which brings lovely compensation in the form of a dozen kinds of tropical fruits. And so *Summer Rainfall* was born, published by Harlequin as Romance #2019 in 1976.

Kerry and her husband run a small electrical-contracting business, and when she isn't writing novels she keeps the company's accounts. When she isn't doing that she helps care for the small herd of cattle and assorted hens that share her acreage.

She and her husband enjoy fishing as a hobby. Another interest is genealogy, largely because her husband's ancestors were among the very earliest settlers to Australia.

Kerry, on the other hand, is a more recent settler; she was born in England and as a child emigrated with her family. Despite her relative newcomer status – or quite possibly because of it–Kerry Allyne writes of Australia and its people with authenticity and love. And it is this spirit of enthusiasm and romance that has won her the loyalty of millions of readers all over the world.

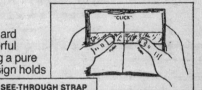

Harlequin reaches into the hearts and minds of women across America to bring you

Harlequin American Romance™

Harlequin American Romance

Twice in a Lifetime
REBECCA FLANDERS

YOURS FREE!